DANCING WITH THE TIDE

HAVE BODY, WILL GUARD ADVENTURE
ROMANCE

BY NEIL S. PLAKCY

This book is a work of fiction. Names, characters, places, and incidents either are products of the author's imagination or are used fictitiously. Any resemblance to actual events or locales or persons, living or dead, is entirely coincidental.

Reviews for Neil Plakcy and the Have Body series:

"Never slows down" – Literary Nymphs Reviews on *Three Wrong Turns in the Desert*

"Plakcy's characters... charm" – Kirkus Reviews

"An engrossing writer" - Publisher's Weekly.

1 — GAME ON

My assailant came at me fast, his right fist clenched, his left arm extended. He was taller than I was, bigger, and stronger, and I felt an adrenaline-laced surge of fear as his beefy arm wrapped around my neck in a choke hold.

But I remembered my lessons, lowered my head so it was below his jaw, then surged upward.

He broke the hold as his head slammed back, and he staggered for a moment. But there was no room for me to escape, and he came at me again, this time keeping his head down. I couldn't help noticing the two brown coins of his nipples against his sleek, bare chest, the way his biceps rippled and his broad shoulders led down to his narrow waist.

He wrapped an arm around me, pulling me close to him again, though keeping my head down. His skin was slippery from oil and sweat, and it was hard to get a purchase on him.

I was shirtless and slippery too, though, and I tried to slide out of his grasp. But he was too quick, and he kicked my legs out from under me. We fell to the faded mat below us, him on top, pinning me to the ground. With one last surge of energy, I brought my knee up to his groin.

"Not that again," he said, moving out of reach at the last minute.

He was focused on my knee, so he wasn't watching my mouth. I grabbed one nipple between my teeth and bit down.

"Oh, you fucker," Liam McCullough said, pulling back, then flopping down next to me on the mat. "You can't turn every fighting lesson into sex play."

"It got you hard," I said, reaching over to stroke his dick through the skimpy nylon shorts we both wore for practice. I could feel the vein that ran down the side of his dick and the mushroom cap, already leaking juice.

"Everything about you gets me hard, Aidan," he said, leaning back against the stucco wall of the living room in the small house we shared. "But if you want to learn to be a bodyguard, you've got to focus on training, not on sex."

"Maybe train some more later." I reached over and skinned down his shorts, letting his stiff dick bang up against his belly. His flesh was hot and smooth, the muscles of his abdomen rippling. I leaned down and licked my tongue up the length of his dick, which made him shiver. He rested his hands on my shoulders – a subtle pressure to let me know he liked what I was doing.

He shivered as I took the head of his dick in my mouth, pursed my lips around it, and inhaled, creating suction. His dick tasted of sweat and the lemon soap we used in the outdoor shower behind our small house, a few blocks off the Avenue Habib Bourguiba in Tunis, the capital of Tunisia.

We had met a few months before, when I fled a failed relationship in Philadelphia and ended up following Liam, a professional bodyguard, into the desert on a crazy adventure. We fell in love against a backdrop of terrorists, camels, and endless sand, and I decided I wanted to be a bodyguard too.

Since my only previous work experience had been teaching English as a Second Language, I had a lot to learn when it came to self-defense, weapons use, and moving silently the way Liam did. I had just returned from a five-day training course in Atlanta, where I renewed my CPR certification, learned defensive-driving skills, demonstrated excellent marksmanship, and studied close-protection tactics.

I didn't need any training, though, when it came to sucking dick. I'd been doing that since I was nineteen, and though I'd been out of practice for a long time, going through a dry spell with my former partner, riding a dick was a lot like riding a bicycle. It came back to you.

Liam sighed deeply as I licked long strokes up and down his dick. I buried my nose in his pubic hair, the rough bristles brushing against my nostrils, and inhaled. I loved Liam's scent. I took one of his big, hairy balls in my mouth and sucked it, then released it and repeated with the other.

"Stop teasing," he panted. "Suck me."

I looked up into his light green eyes and smiled to see the need in them. He was incredibly handsome, from his laughing eyes to his square cheekbones to the light stubble on his chin. Sometimes I looked at him and couldn't believe how lucky I was that this Greek god come to life was my boyfriend.

I wrapped my hand around the base of his dick and felt his

sweat and precome lubricate it. As I sucked and licked and teased the sensitive head, my hand slid up and down on his shaft. Heat rose from his skin, and beads of sweat made glowing tracks down his chest.

He tugged down my shorts and boxers as he rolled me over onto my back, looming above me on his powerful forearms so that I could see every muscle in his naked body rippling. It was one of my favorite positions, though hell, almost every position that involved me and Liam naked was a favorite. He scooted up so that his dick was level with my mouth and began doing push-ups.

Down his dick came into my mouth, driving into my throat. Then he pulled back as he rose above. Down and up, down and up. I grabbed his round, muscular butt cheeks, holding him so that his dick stayed in my mouth, only letting go when I needed to catch my breath.

Feeling his raw power over me was the greatest aphrodisiac. My own dick was stiff and leaking, so hard it was almost painful. Liam shuddered, moaned, and then came in my mouth, the salty fluid dripping down my throat.

Then he lowered his body onto mine. Maybe that was my favorite position -- feeling all his weight on me, the heat rising from his body. He rubbed his belly against my dick, the pressure of his smooth skin grinding against my erection, bringing me off so fast, I couldn't keep up with my own feelings as the passion of my orgasm swept through me. A fire boiled up in my gut and then exploded. I clenched my eyes shut and saw fireworks against my lids. I felt and smelled Liam so close to me that it was like we were one person.

We lay there, enjoying each other's bodies, the Tunisian heat already drying the sweat from our skin. We had pushed the furniture around in the living room to make this impromptu workout area, though sometimes, when it was cooler, we also worked out in the courtyard behind the house, giving the men at the Bar Mamounia across the way a private show.

I was just about to suggest a joint shower when the phone rang. Liam rolled off me and motioned to the iPhone, which sat on the desk, vibrating and rocking to the tune of "Who Let the Dogs Out" by the Baha Men.

"My little secretary," he said as I scrambled up.

"Bigger than you." I did have the bigger dick, though just by an inch, and we had measured each other many times before we finally agreed. What can I say, there's a lot of free-floating testosterone in our relationship, and I wouldn't have it any other way.

At six-four, Liam was three inches taller than I was, with broad shoulders and ropy muscles in his arms and legs. His hair was a light blondish brown, cropped short; mine was darker and shaggier. I had a Mediterranean complexion that was a natural olive, while Liam's skin was deeply tanned from hours in the sun.

"McCullough Protection Associates," I said after noticing the call was a local one from Tunis, from a number I didn't recognize.

The man began speaking quickly in Arabic. I'm good with languages, and I'd started taking Arabic lessons already, but he was much too fast for me. "One moment, please," I interrupted him in

Arabic. I'd learned that much, along with "You are speaking too quickly for me" and "Please hold on."

"You've got to take this one," I said, handing the phone to Liam. "Too much Arabic."

"I have to do everything," he said theatrically, then took the phone from me. "*Aywa,*" he said. That meant yes. "Aywa. Aywa. *Mumkin.*" The last meant "maybe" or "I'll see."

"You want to go to Djerba?" he asked me, holding his hand over the phone. "Bodyguard work?"

Djerba is an island off the coast of Tunisia, renowned for its beaches. "Aywa," I said. "You bet."

He motioned for a pen and paper, which I handed to him, as well as his reading glasses. He looked so sexy there, sitting naked on the rubber mat, a tiny bubble of leftover come dribbling from the top of his soft dick. The half-round reading glasses were an incongruous touch for such a big, strong, handsome man. I could only stare at him and think how lucky I was.

He slipped me a piece of paper with the name "Karif Al-Fulan" and the word "Google." I grabbed my shorts and was about to pull them on when Liam tapped me on the shoulder and shook his head.

Rather than pull a chair up to the simple wooden desk and sit, I stood by the computer, presenting my ass to Liam, and started typing. The top link was to the French-language Tunisian newspaper *La Presse.* My French had always been pretty good, and since moving to Tunis, I had been getting a lot of practice speaking and reading the language, which was the country's second. I scanned the article and said, "Holy shit," as Liam hung up the phone.

"Who is this guy?" he asked, pulling his glasses off and leaning back against the sofa.

"Pop singer. He won the Eurovision song contest a couple of years ago."

"I thought I recognized the name. What's the article say?"

"He came out of the closet two days ago. This morning an imam in Cairo issued a fatwa on him."

Most Westerners, familiar only with Salman Rushdie, thought a fatwa was a death sentence, but for the most part it meant a clerical ruling. In this case, Karif Al-Fulan had been deemed unclean because of his sexual identity. Faithful Muslims were instructed to destroy his records and abstain from listening to his music or attending his concerts.

I read the article out loud, translating relevant parts for Liam, whose French was not as good as mine. I shifted the computer monitor so he could see the picture of Al-Fulan that accompanied the article.

He had a long face, with hazel eyes and skin the color of a very light café Americano, the kind with lots of milk. His black hair draped in sexy curls over his forehead, and he had the hint of a five-o'clock shadow.

As I read and translated, our dog, Hayam, rose from where she had been sleeping and nosed up against Liam's legs, hoping for a treat. He reached down to scratch behind her ears.

Through the open windows, we heard the sounds of a

motorcycle gunning down the street and men laughing in the Bar Mamounia. The air smelled like curry and car exhaust. "Who is it that wants to hire us?" I asked when I was finished.

"Al-Fulan's manager. He called Roberto – you've met him, the Italian guy who handles security at a bunch of nightclubs. He offered the job to Roberto, but the job's too big for him. All he knows how to do is hire bouncers."

Liam preened; after finishing his military service with the US Navy SEALs, he had moved to Tunis and set himself up as a private bodyguard. He had built a clientele slowly, protecting prominent people from kidnapping, assault, assassination, stalking, and so on. He was obviously pleased to get the referral from Roberto.

"What's in Djerba?"

"Private villa owned by the record company. Al-Fulan has gotten some death threats, and he's retreating there. The manager wants someone to keep an eye on him."

Liam crossed his arms over his chest and leaned back against the sofa, his dick nestled in the thatch of his pubic hair. "You sure you're ready to take on a client like this?" he asked. "It's a big job, living in, being on the alert 24-7. If you're not, I can find somebody else to help out, and you can hold down the fort here."

Like I was going to let Liam go off to a private villa with a good-looking gay guy like Karif Al-Fulan. I trusted him -- but I still wondered sometimes at the fate that had brought him to me when he was so gorgeous, with a body built for sex. He laughed at my insecurity, telling me that he loved me and thought I was handsome and that I was the only guy for him. But I still worried.

"I'm in," I said. "How soon do we leave?"

Liam stood up. "This afternoon. We're meeting Al-Fulan and his manager at the Hotel Africa at three. They're chartering a plane to take us to Djerba." He smiled. "Game on."

2 – THREATENING NOTE

While Liam showered, I pulled on my shorts and read everything I could find online about Karif Al-Fulari. He was twenty-five, popular in Tunisia and throughout the Arab world. I watched a YouTube video of his Eurovision-winning song and found myself drawn in. Even though I didn't understand all the words I enjoyed watching him croon to a succession of beautiful young women against a sweeping background of sea and sky.

His official biography said he had been born in Monastir, a seaside town on the Gulf of Hammamet to the south of Tunis. He had been orphaned at twelve and went to live in Tunis with an uncle. He'd begun singing on the streets to earn money, and by the time he was seventeen, he'd moved to Beirut and started performing in nightclubs.

When his debut CD went platinum, he began traveling the Arab world, giving concerts. His second CD had been released to great acclaim, and he had just completed a major tour, which included a series of concerts near the pyramids in Egypt.

"Find anything?" Liam asked, coming into the living room from the backyard shower, drying his hair with a towel, his dick half-hard and hanging to the left.

"There's a hint that there might be compromising photos of him and another man," I said. "That may be what made him come out now."

"We'll have to ask about that. Spurned lovers are always worth investigating."

"I could have figured that out for myself," I said. Liam was still teaching me what he knew about the bodyguard business, but sometimes he treated me like I had no common sense or experience of the world, and that made me cranky.

We were finding our way toward a good working relationship, though. After our return from the desert, I'd helped him with a few cases, standing point or searching for Internet information. I liked the work a lot and liked being with Liam even more. I had decided if I wanted to be Liam's full partner, in love and business, I needed a firmer grasp of executive protection technique and strategy.

I'd begun reading everything I could about the bodyguard business. I had learned a lot from books by a British woman named Zoë Sharp, a series about a female bodyguard working in Britain and the States named Charlie Fox. Then I'd signed up for a weeklong executive protection course in Atlanta.

I hadn't been the best at physical tasks; many of the other guys had been bodybuilders or serious athletes. But I'd gotten the highest marks on any written tests and surprised myself by learning I could shoot almost as well with my left hand as I could with my right.

Most of my classmates had had no real field experience, and I'd entertained them with G-rated stories of my desert adventure with Liam, when we had taken down a remote training school for terrorists.

Liam wrapped his towel around his waist and ran his fingers

through his short brown hair. "What else do you have to do?" he asked. "We've got a lot to accomplish if we're leaving town this afternoon."

"I need to pack and get the house secured, and I want to spend some time searching the gossip Web sites. What are you going to do?"

"I'll do some online recon on the island and what we can expect there while you take your shower," Liam said, motioning toward the courtyard.

"Yes, sir," I said, standing up and saluting. The military effect was muted, though, because I was still naked.

"I like that," Liam said, swatting me on the butt. "A little more obedience, a little less attitude."

"I'll give you attitude," I said, reaching for his towel.

"Go." He picked up his reading glasses and sat at the computer.

I grabbed a towel from the hall closet and walked outside. The first time I had seen Liam, I was in the Bar Mamounia looking out at the courtyard, where he showered under a hose from a cistern on his roof. When I'd moved in with him, the first thing I did was hire a guy to build a simple wooden fence around the shower. I was no exhibitionist, and I had wanted to make a public statement that Liam's naked body would no longer be on display. The patrons of the bar had not been happy.

Even with the fence around me, it gave me a sexual thrill to be showering outdoors. I'd made sure the enclosure was big enough so that Liam and I could share when we wanted, and we'd already made love out there under the broad blue Tunisian sky.

While I was in the shower, Liam pulled on a pair of nylon running shorts and a tank top. By the time I finished, he had downloaded and printed maps and satellite photos of the island, and he had a car rented at Djerba Zarzis airport in Melita.

"Do you know where the flashlights are?" he asked, standing up from the computer and stretching his shoulders. I loved to watch the way his muscles rippled when he did that.

"The plastic hamper on the floor of the bedroom closet. How many days do you think we need clothes for?"

"Make it a week."

I followed him back to the bedroom, my eyes focused on the way his ass moved in his skimpy nylon shorts.

"Put your tongue back in your mouth and get to work," he said, laughing.

He dug through our supplies, pulling out flashlights, maps, night-vision goggles, two-way radios, cell phones, chargers, both our GLOCKs, and a host of other tools. As he laid everything out on his side of the bed, I used my side to put together a pile of shirts, shorts, slacks, and tank tops.

We shared most of our clothes, though our body types were dissimilar. Liam wore tight shirts that stretched across his muscular chest like a second skin, while I was slim and preferred my shirts baggy. We had the same waist size, so I couldn't identify a particular pair of shorts as his or mine.

We couldn't share slacks, as his legs were so much longer than mine. We both favored pants from a US company called 5.11 Tactical, with reinforced knees, ample pockets, and other features that came in handy if you found yourself crawling over rough ground, loaded down with guns, phones, and other tools of the trade.

When it came to underwear, I liked boxers, while Liam stuck to jockstraps and thongs, the skimpier the better. I'd always had locker-room fantasies, and seeing Liam in a fresh white athletic supporter, the pouch cupping his dick, the straps tight against his ass, was enough to make my dick start oozing.

"I'll get Fadi to look after Hayam," Liam said as we were finishing. Our dog was pretty self-sufficient, but whenever we were away, the bartender at the Bar Mamounia made sure she got food and water regularly. "You call the cab."

By two thirty we were en route to the Hotel Africa, one of the biggest and most luxurious hotels in Tunis. I hadn't been inside since I had impersonated a dead guest there, one of the first things I did for Liam.

The lobby looked much the same as it had then; a tracery of Arabic curlicues ran just below the high ceiling, and each of the doorways into other parts of the hotel was surmounted by a pointed arch. The floor was marble, the overstuffed sofas upholstered in dark brown leather. Bright red flowers like oversize poppies, with yellow centers and fringed petals, clustered in vases on the tables.

Liam and I stopped just inside the glass doors, a wall at our back, and surveyed the room. In one corner, an African man in a bright yellow and green dashiki sat hunched over a laptop. A man in a business suit and starched white shirt, with black skin as dark as ebony, paced nearby, a cell phone clasped to his ear.

A bellhop stood next to the concierge desk, while a tourist couple was checking in at the front desk. The left-hand elevator opened, and a middle-aged Arab man in a navy business suit stepped out. He spotted us and crossed the lobby.

We had both dressed to convey our specialties. Liam wore a loose leather vest that showed off his powerful chest and biceps, with drawstring shorts and leather sandals. He was big and muscular, using his physical presence to warn off anyone who thought about messing with him.

I wore khaki slacks and a dark green polo shirt with deck shoes. I was the guy who could blend in with the client. In many situations, you didn't want anyone to know there was a protection specialist present, because it could up the tension level.

In a suit I could sit in on a business meeting or at the next table in a restaurant. In a ball cap and jeans with a sweatshirt to cover the gun at my waist, I could be an ordinary tourist.

The man approached us and immediately began speaking in Arabic to Liam, who stopped him. "You speak English?" he asked. "My associate's Arabic is not as good as mine, and I would like him to hear what you have to say."

"Of course," the man said, his accent heavy but understandable. "I am Yaroush Harootunian, Karif's business manager."

Liam introduced us both. "Come with me," Harootunian said. "Karif is upstairs. He wishes to meet with you before we leave."

As we waited for the elevator, Harootunian said, "This is a terrible thing. I do not know what will happen, but Karif must be safe."

"What kind of threats have you received?" Liam asked.

"Many very bad postings on the Internet," Harootunian said. "Those, not to worry about. A lot of crazy people are out in the world. More troubling are the phone calls to Karif's personal cell phone. This number is not published anywhere."

"Were you able to see the number the calls came from?"

Harootunian shook his head as the elevator arrived and we stepped in. He pushed the button for the fifteenth floor. "The number was blocked."

"I understand there may be some pictures of Mr. Al-Fulan," I said.

"No, no. Karif is not a virgin or a saint, but he has been careful, and there is no one he has been involved with for some time."

As the elevator rose, Harootunian pulled a folded piece of paper from his jacket pocket and handed it to Liam. "This note was delivered to the hotel this morning," he said. "It is why I decided Karif must have protection."

Liam opened the paper, and we both looked at it. Though it was scrawled in Arabic, I recognized the word *mamhoon*, a derogatory word for homosexuals. The other word I recognized was *wafat* -- which meant death.

3 — AIRPORT ROAD

Liam translated the rest for me as the elevator rose. "*Makrooh* means reprehensible," he said, pointing at one word, "and *janabat* means an unclean state caused by sexual intercourse."

He looked at Harootunian. "As far as I can tell, this says that Karif is unclean based on sex acts he has committed, and the only way to cleanse him is death. Close enough?"

Harootunian nodded as the elevator doors opened. We passed a uniformed policeman in the hallway in his pale blue shirt, black slacks, and white cap, then Harootunian led us into the living room of a suite. Two sofas sat perpendicular to floor-to-ceiling windows that looked out at downtown Tunis, with the spire of the Zitouna mosque in the distance. Framed photos of desert scenes hung on the walls, and the carpet was thick enough to camp in.

"The police will only protect Karif for so long," Harootunian said in an undertone as he closed the door behind us. "That is why we must go somewhere safe as soon as possible."

He shepherded us to the sofas and called out, "Karif, I have brought the bodyguards to meet you."

The man who came out of the bedroom was taller than I had expected -- my height, just over six feet. His black hair was tousled, and he had not shaved; there was a haunted look to his eyes as well. But he was just as handsome in person as his pictures had promised. His English was quite good, almost without accent. "You are the bodyguard?" he said, walking to Liam. "Thank you for coming."

I didn't like the way he looked at Liam, his admiring gaze sweeping from Liam's shoulders down to his crotch. I knew Liam dressed the way he did to demonstrate his physical strength, but I still got jealous when someone eyed him hungrily. I had an absurd desire to do something to stake my claim.

We put our bags down on the floor, and Liam introduced himself and me. It wasn't the client's business to know we were lovers as well as coworkers, but I was so accustomed to being out in my past life in Philadelphia that it always made me feel a bit like I was lying not to come clean.

Karif motioned us to sit, his eyes still lasered on Liam. "You can protect me?" he asked.

"Yes," Liam said. "We will secure the property where you'll be staying, monitor who comes and goes, and neutralize any threats."

Karif smiled broadly. "That is very good." To Harootunian, he said, "They will do." Once again he looked wolfishly at Liam.

Many clients saw bodyguards as members of the servant class, there to take care of anything that came up. I'd seen Liam fend off advances from one client's wife and another's daughter. But would he hold on to his principles and keep his dick in his pants when a good-looking man made the overture? I didn't want to risk anything and made a mental vow to keep an eye on Karif Al-Fulan.

As we sat on the overstuffed sofas, Liam asked Harootunian, "You have a place lined up already in Djerba?"

"The record label owns a villa in Mezraia, on the northeast coast, the Zone Touristique. Very private, with its own swimming pool. Karif will wait there until we are able to make sure he can be safe."

"I will be a prisoner there," Karif said, crossing his arms over his chest and pouting. "I have exchanged a closet for a jail cell. This is my freedom."

Liam smiled at him with thin lips, then turned his attention back to Harootunian. "I reserved a car at the airport," he said. "It's better for us to have our own wheels. That way no one knows where we're going."

"The record company will pay. Karif is very valuable to them."

Liam looked at his watch. "Then if we're agreed, are we ready to go?"

"My bag is in the bedroom," Karif said. He rose from the sofa and walked toward the door.

"I'll get it." We were being very well paid for this babysitting job; if it meant I had to carry a suitcase, I didn't mind. Liam went over the contract details with Harootunian as I walked into the bedroom.

The sheets of the king-size bed were tousled, as if Karif had endured a sleepless night. His suitcase was on a luggage rack by the entrance to the bathroom, its contents crumpled and bulging.

I quickly smoothed the shirts and pants, noting that our client wore bikini briefs so tiny, I couldn't imagine they covered much. Then I zipped the case and towed it back to the living room, where Liam was calling downstairs for a bellman. When he arrived, we loaded our bags as well as Karif's and Harootunian's onto the cart. "We'll meet you downstairs," Liam said to the bellman in Arabic.

Once the bellman had gone, Liam stepped out into the hallway and spoke to the policeman on duty. I caught only half the Arabic and figured out the rest as the officer accompanied us in the elevator down to the lobby. The five of us stood crowded together in the small compartment; when we stopped on a lower floor, the policeman held up his hand and told the family there they would have to wait for another car.

Despite the crude message and the threatening phone calls, I wasn't too worried. I'd learned from Liam and my course that most death threats were toothless, intended to sow fear and despair rather than foretell real danger. But Karif Al-Fulan didn't feel the same way. The arrogance he had shown in the suite melted away, and he began to sweat as the elevator descended. He moved close to Liam, and his shoulders shook as the doors opened to the lobby.

I tried not to feel jealous. He was just a scared kid. Of course he would gravitate toward the big, strong bodyguard for protection.

The officer went first, then Harootunian. I put my arm around Karif's shoulders and walked out next to him, with Liam behind us, and I tried to project a sense of calm and control for the client. We moved quickly through the lobby, and I felt attention focused on us like lasers. Conversations stopped, a small boy pointed at us, and a European couple stared. Even the desk clerks stopped what they were doing to watch.

The bellman hailed us the next taxi in the line and loaded the bags in the trunk. As the officer stood next to the vehicle, I got in the backseat and scooted over behind the driver. Harootunian tipped the bellman as Liam directed Karif into the taxi next to me. Once our bags were secure in the trunk, Harootunian got in the backseat too.

Liam was the last to get in, taking the front seat next to the driver, a young guy in a Rolling Stones T-shirt. The driver waved to the bellman and pulled into the Avenue Habib Bourguiba.

I noticed that a black Toyota pulled out behind our cab. But it's not unusual to see cars tailgating one another or speeding past, darting in and out of traffic as if the drivers were practicing for Indianapolis. The Avenue Habib Bourguiba was a busy street, with six lanes of traffic separated by a thick verge of trees in the center, and there were bound to be cars all around us.

Karif began arguing with Harootunian in Arabic. I couldn't follow most of the conversation, though I could tell from Liam's body language he was listening closely. I got the feeling that Karif didn't want to go to Djerba; he thought he would be safer in Britain or America. Harootunian didn't agree; they had no contacts in either place, he said, and the record label wanted Karif to stay close.

The black Toyota remained a few car lengths behind us as we drove through heavy traffic toward the city center. Motorcycles and tour buses competed with passenger sedans and taxis for space in the narrow streets. I lost sight of the black Toyota, and I thought we'd lost it, but when the cab turned onto the P9 toward the airport, it was behind us again.

I thought about mentioning it to Liam. But he was so focused on the argument between Karif and his manager that I didn't want to disturb him. As we approached the turn for the airport, the black

Toyota accelerated, gaining rapidly on us. Our cab driver was nodding along to the internal soundtrack in his head, taking the turn, when the Toyota pulled up on our left and tried to force him off the road.

"Liam!" I said. "Black Toyota, nine o'clock." I turned my body to the window, wrapped my arm around Karif, and pushed him toward the floor, shielding him from possible gunfire.

The cabbie erupted in a stream of Arabic invective as he wrestled the wheel, slipping away from the Toyota at the last minute, making the turn and leaving the Toyota skidding into the grassy median.

"What was that?" Harootunian demanded of me as I helped Karif get up. "Was that an assassination attempt?"

The driver was shouting, and Liam tried to calm him down and direct him to the private terminal where our charter flight waited. Karif shook like the leaves of a palm in the desert sirocco. I patted his shoulder as I said to Harootunian, "Probably just bad driving. But with our nerves on edge, it seemed worse."

Liam caught my eye. I could tell that wasn't what he thought, but he was happy I'd tried to calm the client rather than aggravate the situation. The driver argued the rest of the way to the terminal, and he only shut up when Harootunian handed him a sheaf of bills.

The breeze coming in from the Gulf of Tunis did little more than wash hot, heavy air over us as we walked to the Tunisavia departure lounge in a one-story building with a corrugated metal roof. It reverberated with the sound of jets taking off and landing nearby.

A young guy in a shirt with the Tunisavia logo of a stylized bird in flight came to meet us and arranged for our bags to be transferred from the cab to the plane. Karif was still shaky on his feet, and I had to keep my arm around him as the Tunisavia rep led us into a large room with open windows and a couple of lazy overhead fans.

"We have a twenty-passenger DeHavilland Twin Otter ready for you," he said. "I will need some signatures, and then we will have you on your way."

A young woman in a matching Tunisavia shirt brought us bottles of cold water, and Karif huddled with his in the center of a row of molded plastic seats. While Harootunian signed the necessary forms, Liam pulled me aside. We stepped over to the big windows that overlooked the tarmac.

A dark-skinned man in a T-shirt and shorts loaded our bags into the back of a small jet with large call numbers painted on its fuselage and a staircase extended from the door. "What did you see?" Liam asked in a low voice.

I looked over my shoulder at Karif. He leaned forward and clutched the water bottle. "A black Toyota pulled out after us when we left the hotel. I can't be certain it's the same one that tried to knock us off the road."

"Why didn't you say anything? We can't work together effectively if we don't communicate."

The building shook with the reverberation of a jet passing overhead. "I'm well aware we have to share information with each other, Liam. You don't have to talk to me like a child. You were busy listening to Karif and Yaroush argue. And besides, I didn't want to worry the client."

"I'm sorry. I didn't mean to make it sound like you did something wrong. You're right, saying something in front of Yaroush and Karif would have upset them even more. But we could have been better prepared if we had known about the black Toyota earlier."

"You're right. But it wasn't a danger until the driver made his move." I knew I sounded petulant and that it was our responsibility to anticipate problems, not just react to them. But I still didn't have enough confidence in my own skills, and I tended to second-guess myself too much.

"We're going to have to be on guard from now on," Liam said. "There may be some real substance to these threats."

4 – PRIVATE VILLA

I'd never been on a chartered plane before, but I had always expected them to be nicer. This one was ratty around the edges -- no carpet on the floor, stains on the seat covers. There were six rows of seats, singles on one side of the aisle, doubles on the other. Not the lap of luxury, but as long as the engine worked, I was okay with it.

The pilot was a portly man in his fifties, with skin the color of weak tea and a white shirt that was too tight around the neck. He repeated his welcome to us in Arabic, French, and heavily accented English. His copilot -- who looked barely out of his teens -- doubled as a flight attendant; once we had taken off, he came into the cabin and handed out more bottles of water, along with peanuts and granola bars.

"The flight is not long to Djerba Zarzis airport," he said. "The captain will keep the seat belt sign on because we will not go very high at all."

We arced out over the Gulf of Tunis, then turned south, crossing the peninsula that ended in Cape Bon. We flew so low that I saw houses and farms below us, the occasional car or truck crawling around the base of a mountain that rose out of the plains. When we reached the Gulf of Hammamet, we began to follow the coastline. Below us, waves crashed against a long strip of sandy beach. I saw a couple of surfers down there, dancing with the waves, and envied them that joy and freedom.

I imagined us frolicking on a beach like that, the client in the water, perhaps, Liam and me stretched out on the sand, relaxed but alert. We had just finished a very stressful case the week before, protecting the daughter of a wealthy family while her divorce from an abusive husband was finalized. The man had made numerous threats against his wife and her family, and we had to be constantly on the alert. The case ended when her father paid the ex a lot of money to leave Tunisia and start over again in Canada.

We could both use the break after that case, and I hoped that this job would turn out to be little more than babysitting, despite that near accident on the road to the airport.

I looked across the plane at Karif. His agitation had been replaced with a sort of catatonia. He slumped in a window seat, staring forward. Liam sat next to him, speaking in a low voice, reaching out to put a hand on his knee. I sat across the aisle and one behind, trying not to notice the way Karif shifted closer to Liam and rested his head on Liam's tanned shoulder.

I reminded myself that Liam was treating Karif as a VIP client. By the time we crossed into the Gulf of Gabès and prepared for our approach to Djerba Zarzis airport, Karif was laughing at some joke Liam had made, and the atmosphere inside the plane lifted.

The white arcs of kite-surfer sails blossomed below us against a backdrop of bright blue ocean water. Small fishing boats rocked in the current in the tiny bays that ringed the island. I struggled to keep a vision in my mind of a nice vacation, a few days in a luxury villa with swimming and water sports.

When we landed, we climbed out of the plane to temperatures that were at least ten degrees cooler than in Tunis. There was hardly a cloud in the sky, and the sun was bright but not blinding. Liam and Harootunian went off to get the rental car, and Karif and I walked into the beautiful new terminal, with its huge arched windows and hanging red pennants. We could have been in any large city in Europe, surrounded as we were by couples and families on holiday. The chatter around us was a mix of French, German, and Arabic.

"Do you think someone tried to kill me in Tunis?" Karif asked as we walked toward the terminal exit, trailed by a skycap with our bags on a cart.

"I don't know. I've seen a lot of lousy driving since I moved here."

"You are from America?"

"Philadelphia," I said, nodding.

"I would like to go to America." Karif crossed his arms over his chest. "Yaroush, he tries to organize tour for me. We are thinking now that I am out of closet, maybe I can get gay men to like my singing."

"I'm sure they would. You are handsome and young. Liam and I have never heard you sing, though. Maybe you will sing for us sometime?"

"He is your boyfriend?"

Liam and I had talked about this when he had agreed I could join him in his bodyguard business. He thought it was best that we present ourselves as associates rather than lovers. Homosexuality was a problem in many Arab countries; in Tunisia, for example, anal sex was against the law, and Liam knew of men who had been prosecuted. Though there were clandestine gay bars and a growing sense of tolerance among the educated and less religious, it was best to be quiet.

Before coming to Tunisia, I had taught English as a Second Language to immigrants in Philadelphia, and I'd always been out in my professional life. I thought it was important to be a role model for gay students. I also wanted to educate those who had come to the United States from less tolerant cultures that gay people were part of American society, and they had better learn to get along with us.

I could lie to Karif, I thought. But he wasn't stupid, and we'd be living with him for the next few days. I didn't relish the thought of hiding during that time. And I presumed we had been hired because someone, somehow, knew we were gay and would be sympathetic to Karif's problems.

"Yes, he's my boyfriend," I said.

"He is very handsome. His chest!"

I smiled, and Karif said hurriedly, "You are also, of course. I did not mean to say that you were not."

"Thank you," I said as we came to the terminal exit doors, where I looked both ways, evaluating any potential dangers. The first few times I'd done this exercise with Liam in Tunis and then in Atlanta, I had felt foolish, like a kid playing a game, but seeing my classmates struggle to master the skills and hearing stories from my instructors made me believe it had to be done.

Cabs waited in line to our left, while a tour bus sat idling to our right. I couldn't see beyond the bus, though, so I decided it would be better for us to wait inside. I directed Karif toward a flat, illustrated guide to the island mounted on a waist-high pedestal to our right. The skycap dropped our luggage next to it, and I tipped him.

"You have been to Djerba before?" Karif asked.

I shook my head. "Have you?"

"My record company, they have this house. I have been there once, twice before."

He studied the island map as I looked around. A tour group was checking in at the Tunisair platform; a woman in a body-cloaking light blue burka squatted next to a small boy and tried to get him to stop crying. Sunburned tourists crossed behind us, and the loudspeaker repeated the same phrases in Arabic, French, and English.

I looked uneasily out through the high glass windows. How long would it take Liam to get the car? "I would like to ride a quad bike," Karif said, pointing at one of the ads on the map.

"We're getting a car," I said. "For all four of us."

"Not from the airport. When we are at the villa. There is a rental office down the beach."

"We'll see." I didn't know what a quad bike was, but it didn't sound like something Liam would think was safe.

"I am the person in charge. If I want to try a quad bike, I will."

"You are the client," I said, trying not to sound cranky. "That doesn't mean you are in charge. Your record company hired us to protect you, and Liam is the expert. If you want to stay alive, you'll listen to him."

Karif glared at me, then turned to look outside. Just as I heard Liam on the two-way radio, Karif spotted the car. "There!" he said. "Yaroush is waving at us."

He took off toward the front door. "Karif! Wait!" I yelled, running after him. I grabbed his arm. "Wait here until Liam comes in. He'll take you outside, and I'll bring the bags."

Karif didn't like being told what to do. I radioed Liam and asked him to come inside, and Karif waited, his arms crossed. I turned sideways, keeping my eye on our bags by the map, and on Karif, until Liam reached him.

By the time I dragged all the bags out to the Land Rover Liam had rented, he was in the driver's seat, Karif next to him. Yaroush was in the backseat. I loaded all the bags, then slid in next to him, sweat dripping down my forehead and pooling under my arms.

"You do what is required to keep your client safe," one of my teachers in Atlanta, a man with a long résumé that included rock stars, actors, and sports heroes, had lectured. "If you must jog with him or carry his bags or wait outside in the heat or cold to be sure the area is safe, you do it."

I scanned the road as we left the airport. If anything happened to Liam, I might have to get Karif back to the airport, so I had to know the way. And with Liam focused on directions, it was important that I pay attention to any possible threats. The two-lane blacktop road was edged by short and tall palm trees, with sand and scrub stretching off in both directions. The land was flat, and the sky looked like it stretched on forever.

Centuries before, Djerba had been a sanctuary for corsairs and pirates, but this road, at least, was a bad spot for an ambush, because we could see cars coming from quite a distance, and there was no place to hide for miles. As we neared the center of Melita, the white stucco houses called *menzels* sprouted from the land as organically as the date palms. We stopped to let a farmer lead three camels across the road in front of a large menzel that looked like a collection of blinding white blocks stacked together. One block was covered with a rough dome, while an outside staircase led to the flat roof of an attached cube. A giant aloe bloomed in the sandy front yard, and in the shaded courtyard, a small boy sat on the ground watching us with interest.

As we approached the main town of Houmt Souk, Liam took a right turn to curve around the town to the edge of the Mediterranean, where we picked up the coast road. Hotel followed hotel, with stretches of gorgeous sandy beaches and blue-green water. Male and female tourists in tiny bikinis lounged in the sand or sat on terraces sipping colorful drinks. I kept having to remind myself that danger could be around the next curve despite the holiday atmosphere.

We drove all the way through Mezraia until we reached a narrow dirt road which led to the white stucco Villa Palma. Two stories tall with a tile roof, it looked like something out of *Architectural Digest*, with an arched doorway, clerestory windows, and a half-round wrought-iron balcony that looked toward the ocean.

Liam drove up the winding drive and stopped in front of gates set in a six-feet-high stone wall. "Is very secure," Yaroush said, leaning forward. "Many times, famous recording artists come here." He gave Liam the code for the keypad, and the gates swung open.

"This wall runs the perimeter of the property?" Liam asked.

"Yes," Yaroush said. "Is an intercom from the kitchen to open gate."

Liam pulled up in front of a garage on the right side of the house. "Remote control for garage door is in kitchen also," Yaroush said.

We piled out of the Land Rover into the bright sun and heat of midday. In the distance I could see the ocean and barely hear the rush of waves and the occasional car or motorcycle passing below. The small yard had been landscaped with sand and cacti, and a white stone path led to the front door.

"I want to walk around the perimeter of the property," Liam said.

"I will go with you," Karif said. "Come." He tugged on Liam's hand, and they set off toward the front gate.

I resisted the impulse to swat the client's hand away from my boyfriend and started unloading the bags as Yaroush popped out his cell phone and made a call. I was getting accustomed to the role of Sherpa porter, though grudgingly.

The villa's living room was a high-ceilinged space with white stucco walls, a beige carpet, and dark brown leather sofas and easy chairs. The paintings on the walls looked like they'd been chosen by a corporate decorator -- brilliant splashes of color that balanced the desert tones.

An air conditioner hummed in the background, and the cool air was a relief after the outdoor heat. I left Karif's bags in the master bedroom, which looked out over the ocean and had its own Roman tub with Jacuzzi. It resembled a high-end hotel room, with dark furniture and a striped spread and satin throw pillows on the king-size bed. The curtains over the sliding-glass doors to the balcony had been pulled back, exposing a broad vista of ocean and beach. The bright Tunisian sun spilled into a warm puddle on the intricately patterned Oriental rug.

Yaroush followed me upstairs, his phone still at his ear. "You will want this room," he said, opening the door to a large room across the hall that looked out at the pool; it had two queen-size beds and its own bathroom as well. Shutters on the windows had been pulled half-closed, letting in stripes of light.

The decorator's hand was evident here too in the way all the colors of the room complemented each other. I preferred a more personal touch, feeling a room should be unified by the personality of the resident rather than a carefully orchestrated palette. But I wasn't buying the place, just staying there for a few days.

Yaroush finished his call and snapped the phone shut. "I will take this one," he said, opening a third door. The room was small, and the shutters had been pulled closed. "I am only staying a short time."

"You are?"

"I must go to business in Rome," he said. "I will fly tomorrow, after I see that Karif is safe."

He led me back to the kitchen, where I found a mind-numbing list of instructions for everything from the gate intercom to wireless Internet to the microwave oven. "There is caretaker," Yaroush said. "Hakim maintain property, his wife, Alisa, is maid. Here is phone number if you have emergency."

Hakim had been there already, leaving the refrigerator and freezer stocked with food. Yaroush went off to make more phone calls, and I was evaluating the dinner possibilities when Liam and Karif came inside, laughing and mock fighting. I didn't like the way Karif took every opportunity to put his hands on Liam. He might be the client, but that didn't give him any privileges with my boyfriend.

"We're going to go swimming," Liam said to me. "You'll get comfortable with all the house systems?"

"Sure," I said, noticing I hadn't been invited to join them. "I put the bags upstairs in the bedrooms. Your bathing suit is in the brown duffle."

"We have no need for bathing suit," Karif said. "We are all men here."

"You're the client," Liam said, laughing. "Come on. Let's go."

As I configured our laptop computer to work with the house's network, I looked out the kitchen window at the pool, where Liam and Karif, both naked, frolicked in the water. Liam's body was deeply tanned except for a white triangle usually covered by the bikini suit he liked, while Karif was dark all over. The two of them dived and wrestled and played while I worked, which made me even crankier.

I reminded myself that it was our job to keep Karif safe, and if that meant making sure he was happy to hang around the villa instead of renting quad bikes or cruising the bars of Mezraia and Houmt Souk, then we were getting paid very well for work that wasn't all that hard.

When the computer was hooked up, I identified all the phones, mastered the codes for the intercom, and unpacked my bag and Liam's. I looked out the bedroom window and saw Liam and Karif had left the pool and were splayed out on lounge chairs in the sun. It was time for this Cinderfella to go to the ball, I thought. I'd done all my chores, and I deserved some fun.

I found three big beach towels in the hall closet, then stripped down. It felt funny to walk through the house naked, but I was confident that my body was as good as Karif's, if not as muscular as Liam's.

My dick was semihard as I prepared to open the sliding-glass door to the patio area. I couldn't help it; thinking of Liam does that to me.

I could see he was having that effect on Karif too. Our client was fully hard, his dick wagging in the air as he stood under the shower by the pool. Liam was next to him, both of them washing off the chlorine. The sun was brilliant, glittering off something shiny inland of the villa. A cluster of birds soared on high thermals, their wings outstretched. As one of them swooped past, I realized it was a hawk, searching for prey, and that reminded me that there were people out there who would hurt our client if they could.

I looked from the sky back to the shower. As I watched, unseen by either of them, Karif leaned up and kissed Liam.

My erection wilted, and I dropped the towels on the floor, then bolted upstairs.

5 – LIAM MULTITASKS

I felt like I was going to throw up, so I made for the bathroom, passing a startled Yaroush Harootunian in the hallway. Nothing would come up, but I felt tears trickling down my face.

No matter where we went, men and women were attracted to Liam, and I couldn't help but be jealous, even though he insisted he wasn't tempted by anyone but me. I felt so connected to him, and I believed him. The possibility that I'd been wrong tore away at my insides.

Liam had fought his attraction to men as a teenager, through college, and into his training as a US Navy SEAL. From what I understood, his only sexual contacts with other men had been casual one-night stands, furtive gropings in bars and restrooms. He'd never been able to believe he could have a true relationship with another man until he met me in Tunis.

He said I was the first man he ever loved. Though we argued over little things like wet towels on the bedroom floor, or big things like client tactics, we said "love you" to each other a few times a day - - waking up, going out, just before bed. I had been in relationships before, including an eleven-year stint that had broken up just before I met Liam. I knew how magical and special the connection we had was.

"Aidan?" Liam knocked on the bathroom door. "Sweetheart?"

"Go away."

"Aidan. Don't be a child. Open the door."

I sighed, reached over and unlocked the door, then leaned back against the vanity. My stomach was in knots, and tears streaked my cheeks.

Liam opened the door and stepped into the lavish bathroom with me. He'd wrapped a towel around his waist, and his chest glistened with droplets of water. "Come here," he said. He wrapped his arms around me and pulled me close to him. "You saw that, didn't you?"

I didn't say anything, just nodded my head against his chest.

"I backed away as soon as he kissed me," Liam said. "I told him I was already taken. By you."

"Really?" I looked up at him.

"Really." He leaned down and kissed me. Even though I was nearly six-one, Liam still had almost four inches on me. I loved that about him, the sense that he was bigger and stronger than I was, that he would protect me from anything the world threw at us.

"I love the way you get jealous," Liam said. "It shows me you care about me. And believe me, baby, I feel just the same way. If Karif had chosen you to kiss, I'd be ready to punch him in the stomach." He leaned back. "But you have to remember, this is a job, and he's the client. It's a matter of setting the boundaries. I made it clear to him how things stand. He just didn't know we were a couple."

"He knew. He asked me while we were waiting for you to get the rental car."

"He asked you if we were gay?"

"Yes."

He backed away a foot and crossed his arms. "I thought we talked about that. Our private life is nobody else's business. If word gets around that we're gay, what do you think that's going to do to our reputation?"

"Get a grip, Liam. Why do you think we got this job, after all? Why didn't they go to one of the bigger agencies with more resources?"

"Because no one else wanted the job," Liam said.

"Really? Because the client is gay? What about the security for the Elton John concert in Tunis? You think Meridian Associates didn't realize he was as queer as a three-dollar bill?"

"That's different."

"How? You think they were scared off by the fact that Karif got a couple of nasty phone calls?"

Liam was a smart guy, but sometimes he could be really dense. I saw confusion on his face as he processed the information. "So you're saying Yaroush knew we were gay before he hired us?"

"I think so. And that means somebody had to tell him. Most likely somebody else in the private security business."

"Shit."

"Does it matter, Liam?"

"You saw the threats Karif got. You've seen the way the Arab world looks at faggots like us. Of course it matters."

"So fuck 'em all. We'll prove we can be gay and great

bodyguards. We're a terrific team, and if a client doesn't want to hire us, it's their loss."

He smiled. "Yeah, I guess you're right."

"Of course I am," I said, pulling him close to me. His towel came loose as we snuggled, and his dick rose. So did mine. He lifted me onto the marble vanity, and I shivered as my skin met the cold stone. "Let me warm you up," he said, dropping to his knees.

My dick was hard by the time he rubbed his cheek against it, the roughness chafing. "You know I love you, don't you?" he asked, looking up at me.

"I know. And I love you too."

He licked his tongue up the length of my dick, and electric tremors ran through my body. *How do you like this, Karif?* I thought, as Liam swallowed me down to the root, then pulled back up, sucking like a vacuum cleaner.

Karif. Who was looking after Karif?

"Honey," I said as Liam nibbled lightly at the mushroom head of my dick, "who's watching the client?"

"Yaroush," he said, looking up at me. "I told him we needed a couple of minutes."

I should have known, I thought, leaning back on my hands and letting Liam suck me. He was a professional. He wouldn't have ducked into the bathroom for a quickie without making sure the client was protected. We'd learned that in bodyguard school, although not exactly in those terms.

Liam sucked dick like he did everything else -- with passion, with dedication, with talent. He reached one hand under my balls and tickled the tip of my ass crack as he sucked me. The other snaked up to tweak one of my nipples.

He was like that guy in high school who could rub his stomach and pat his head at the same time -- a true multitasker. He began bobbing his head up and down on my dick, faster and faster, and my orgasm raged through my body. I struggled to hold back the cries and yelps I usually made, worrying that Yaroush or Karif would be outside the door listening.

Squinting my eyes closed, grimacing my lips together, I let loose a stream of come into Liam's mouth, and my whole body went limp. Liam stood up, licked his lips lasciviously, and leaned back against the bathroom door, his stiff dick waving. He looked at me, then looked down at himself.

I hopped off the bathroom counter, laid a bath mat at his feet, and knelt down. Liam's dick was a thing of beauty, as far as I was concerned. Just above average in length and girth, it was more than a mouthful, big enough to fill me up front or back without overwhelming me. That morning it tasted like chlorine and sunshine. I swallowed him all the way, feeling his pubic hair tickle my nose, then began bobbing up and down.

"Oh yeah," Liam groaned as I reached a finger up and began playing with his ass, teasing the fine hairs around the opening. He grabbed my head and began pushing me down on his dick. While I had it in my mouth, I tickled it with my tongue, and he groaned again.

I backed off, using as much suction as I could muster, and felt his dick swelling and throbbing and knew he was close. I pushed my index finger straight up his ass, and the muscles locked around me -- and then he erupted, spurting hot come down my throat.

By the time we left the bathroom, Karif had gone into his bedroom for a nap. Yaroush was on the phone in the living room, and I went into the kitchen to fix us all some dinner, feeling very satisfied. Hakim had left fresh shrimp in the refrigerator, and I skewered it along with green peppers, mushrooms, and cherry tomatoes. I figured out how to use the fancy rice cooker, then warmed up flatbread and lathered it with goat cheese as an appetizer.

Liam uncorked a bottle of Italian white wine, we called in Karif and Yaroush, and I slid the skewers under the oven broiler. Yaroush put one of Karif's CDs on the stereo, and we all sat down at the dining room table. Karif had a full-bodied tenor, and the first song showed his range. I loved the swirling sound of the saxophone in the background, the rhythm of the drums.

Karif pouted through the meal, sitting with his arms crossed. He refused the appetizer, then tasted the shrimp and called them overdone, even though I thought they were juicy and perfect. Liam and I talked to Yaroush about Karif's career, the places he had performed, and how well his CDs had sold. Karif only answered direct questions from Yaroush, with a yes or no.

"I want to go out," Karif said when the CD finished and we were left without background noise. "I want to go to a club."

"That's not a good idea," Liam said. "At least not for a few days.

You should lie low until we know exactly what your situation is."

Karif slammed his hand against the wooden table. "My situation is that I am stuck in this villa hiding when I should be out enjoying myself, making love with many handsome men!"

Yaroush and Liam frowned, but I understood Karif's frustration. I had come out of the closet my freshman year in college, and I had been determined to get laid as often as possible. That only worked out to once every other month or so, but at least I hadn't been shut up somewhere. As I fixed cappuccinos for us, I ran through things we could do to get Karif's mind off sex.

I said, "Why don't I clean up while you guys play some pool?"

"No," Karif said.

"Come on," Liam said. "I can show you some moves. It'll be fun."

Karif agreed grudgingly, and Liam led him to the pool table. Yaroush excused himself to look over some contracts upstairs, and I cleaned up. When I was finished, I peeked into the den. Karif leaned over the table, pointing the cue at a striped ball, Liam just behind him, his hand on Karif's. Liam said something in Arabic, and Karif laughed. My heart flip-flopped, but I was determined not to overreact. I stood in the shadows watching as Karif lined up his shot, and Liam stepped back. Karif knocked the striped ball into the corner pocket, and he and Liam high-fived.

I could have joined them, lounging in the corner watching the game. But I trusted Liam more than that. Instead I climbed up to our bedroom, where I picked up the guidebook and read that it was believed the beautiful women of Djerba had fed Ulysses and his crew lotus flowers, and the men were so pleasantly intoxicated Ulysses found it tough to make them return to their ships.

Well, that wasn't the Djerba I'd seen so far, but maybe that would change. It was a pretty island, with charming towns and gorgeous beaches, but I wasn't intoxicated yet. There were supposed to be more than a million date palms and hundreds of thousands of olive trees on the island, making it one giant oasis.

I read about each of the towns on the island, their markets and their specialties, and around eleven o'clock I started to feel sleepy. Liam still had not come up to bed, though, so I crept downstairs to see what he and Karif were up to.

It was sneaky to move so quietly, as if I hoped to surprise the two of them doing something a lot worse than kissing, but I couldn't help myself. I trusted Liam -- but I didn't trust Karif at all.

They had given up on pool and were sitting in the living room, on sofas across from each other, drinking from a bottle of Greek ouzo. As I watched from the staircase, I noticed Liam's glass was still full as he refilled Karif's. Satisfied, I went back to the bedroom and went to sleep.

6 – A Broken Vase

The next morning I left Liam sleeping on his back, his mouth open, snoring, and checked on Karif. He was sprawled on his bed, naked and uncovered, his chest rising and falling with each breath. I was pleased to note his dick was smaller than average.

Yaroush Harootunian was still asleep in his small room too. I walked through the whole house, then checked the perimeter. When I was confident that everything was secure, I went into the kitchen and started brewing coffee and baking some breakfast rolls, and Yaroush came down to join me.

"They are sleeping off the ouzo?" he asked, hoisting the nearly empty bottle.

"Yes. I hope Karif is in a better mood this morning."

"He will not be happy when I leave," Yaroush said.

"Does he know you're not staying?"

Yaroush shook his head. "Sometimes he is still a boy, you know. I only tell him what he needs to know."

I decanted a cappuccino for him from the machine and started frothing the milk. "How long have you been his manager?" I asked over the noise.

"Four years now. When I meet Karif, he is singing in club in Beirut."

"He has a beautiful voice," I said, remembering the CD we had heard the night before.

"Like an angel, that one," Yaroush said. "Voice of an angel, I mean."

I handed him the cappuccino, and he poured sugar into it and stirred. "You're saying he doesn't behave like an angel?"

Yaroush shrugged. "He is a boy. He had hard life before, so now he likes to have his way."

Great. Our client was a spoiled kid just out of the closet who had a lot of hard times to make up for.

"I cannot be his father," Yaroush said. "But he needs strong man, you know. Good influence. I am thinking you and your partner will help him."

"You mean help him with his coming out?" I remembered my conversation with Liam the day before. "Did you hire us because we're gay?"

Yaroush shifted in his chair. "I look for agencies to protect Karif. I call couple of places. They do not want case."

That surprised me. There weren't a lot of companies that specialized in executive protection in Tunisia; quite often visiting dignitaries and celebrities came with their own staff. I figured that the couple of agencies we competed with would be happy for any kind of work. Maybe Liam was right, and he and I should be more circumspect about our private lives. Or perhaps we could make a specialty out of protecting gay clients in the Arab world.

"Because Karif came out of the closet?" I asked. "Or because of the danger?"

Yaroush shrugged. "I did not interrogate them. I wanted people who would protect Karif. One man told me that you and Liam were more than just business partners. He would not say more, but I understood him."

"We will do our best to protect Karif. Because we are professionals. Not for any other reason."

Yaroush looked up at me and smiled. "That is very good."

Liam came downstairs, yawning and rubbing the sleep from his eyes. He wore only a pair of nylon running shorts, and once again I was struck by how perfect his body was, like Michelangelo's *David* come to life. Square pecs tapered to a narrow waist, his nipples two brown circles against his tan flesh. His biceps were so well-defined they could have come from an anatomy text.

The nylon shorts clung to his body like a second skin, and they were short enough to expose his muscular thighs, strong enough to hold me in a vise grip. His only imperfection were his toes; the second ones on each foot were strangely long, and his pinkie toes turned outward.

At home I loved his casual nudity, because we were by ourselves and I enjoyed the view. But it was a different story when there were clients involved. I was about to say something, tell him to put a shirt on, for Christ's sake, but remembered his dictum about behavior in front of clients.

He took a cappuccino gratefully from me and slid into a chair. I put aside my irritation and began to clean the machine.

"One of you can drive me to the airport?" Yaroush asked. "I have flight to Rome at eleven."

"I can do it," Liam said. "I want to check out the island in case we decide it's safe for Karif to go out."

We ate in a companionable silence, and when we finished, Yaroush rose from the table and said, "I must tell Karif I am going."

After he went upstairs, I said to Liam, "Do you think you could put some clothes on in front of the clients?"

"Oh come on, Aidan. Let's not start that again," Liam said. "I'm not interested in sex with Karif. Get over yourself and move on."

"It's not about sex," I said. "It's about what's appropriate. Aren't you the one who says we have to be professional around our clients? Doesn't that mean dressing properly?" I was wearing a polo shirt and a pair of cargo shorts. I was even wearing sandals, though I preferred to be barefoot in the house.

"You've got a stick up your butt this morning."

"Don't avoid the question, Liam."

He drained the last of his cappuccino and looked at me. "You're right. I should have gotten dressed before I came downstairs." He held up his hand and said, "And before you get into it, yes, I shouldn't have gotten naked in the pool with Karif yesterday either. But this isn't your traditional assignment, and I think we both need to be more flexible."

"Flexible how?"

He shrugged. "I don't know. I'm making it up as I go along. Within limits I think it's good for Karif to feel like he's on vacation with a couple of friends, not like he's locked up in prison with armed guards. Yes, he needs to realize he has to listen to us, that we know how to protect him. But a little skinny-dipping, some pool playing, a couple of drinks -- I think we can manage that."

"How late did you stay up last night?"

He yawned. "Just midnight or so. Fortunately Karif can't hold his liquor very well. I had to carry him upstairs and put him to bed."

I remembered looking in on Karif, finding him naked. "About that," I said, but my thought derailed when we heard a crash from upstairs.

Liam was quicker than I was, sprinting out of the kitchen, then up the stairs, but I was just behind him. By the time I got to the master bedroom, I heard Karif yelling in Arabic. I couldn't make out the exact words, but I could tell he wasn't happy that Yaroush was leaving him. I caught the word *mamhoon*, that derogatory term for gay, but it took me a minute to realize Karif wasn't talking about himself -- but about Liam and me.

It's one thing for a straight person to use a term like that in a negative way, but for a gay person to complain about faggot bodyguards really pissed me off. Liam walked into the bedroom, and I stood in the doorway.

Harootunian cowered against one wall as Karif, still buck naked, aimed a lamp at him. On the floor I saw the smashed remains of what looked like a vase of flowers and an alarm clock.

"That's enough," Liam said as he walked toward Karif. Karif threw the lamp at him, but Liam caught it one-handed, then set it down on the floor. Karif lunged at him, throwing punches, but Liam enfolded the boy singer in his arms.

I knew he was doing it to calm Karif down and keep him from causing more damage, but I was still jealous. There was nothing better for me than cuddling up next to Liam, his strong arms wrapped around me. My head resting against his muscular chest, feeling his heartbeat. Just the thought of it made my dick stiffen, and I had to resist the impulse to pry Karif away.

"It's all right," Liam said as Karif's punches subsided and he began to cry. The singer's dark head rested against Liam's tanned chest, and Liam rubbed his back. "Aidan and I are here. We're going to take care of you."

I wasn't close enough to see if contact with Liam had the same effect on Karif as it did on me, and that was good. I didn't want to know if our client's dick was stiff and pressed against Liam's thigh through the thin nylon of Liam's shorts.

Yaroush ducked out to retrieve his suitcase, and Liam convinced Karif to get back in bed. He leaned over the boy, tucking the covers up to his neck, and kissed his forehead. As we backed away, Karif closed his eyes and rested against the pillow.

Liam took me aside as Yaroush was carrying his bag out to the Land Rover. "You're in charge here," he said. "Don't let the little shit push you around."

"Little shit, huh?" I asked. "Not cute, sexy boy toy?"

"Absolutely not. I'm attracted to men, not whiny little boys. And in case you didn't know, I'm attracted to you."

He pulled me close for a kiss, his rough lips touching mine with just the lightest pressure. I closed my eyes and focused on the sensation of his cheek against mine, the heat rising from his chest, the smell of him next to me. All too soon he pulled away.

"Gotta go," he said. "But I'll be back soon."

7 – SEXUAL TENSION

As Karif slept, I opened up the laptop and connected to the Internet. I wanted to see what kind of buzz his declaration was getting online and in the media. I couldn't find much in any of the English-language search engines, and I thought that was a good sign. There was so much going on in the Arab world that the media had, for the most part, moved on. The president of France was brokering a new agreement between several factions in Palestine, trying to organize a coalition government. Fundamentalist militants had bombed a tourist hotel in Dubai, and a persistent drought in Egypt had left Lake Nasser at record low levels.

When I'd lived in Philadelphia, I paid little attention to international news except as it related to my students. Floods in Haiti might mean Guerly St. Jean would be worried about his family; Minh Ly obsessed over every story about her homeland, Vietnam; and political unrest in Honduras stressed Alejandro Trujillo. I knew the geography of the African and Arab worlds, but for the most part my eyes glazed over at the latest reports of famine in Sudan or tsunami in Indonesia.

Now that I lived in Tunisia, though, these stories had much more impact. Liam had been hired to escort a Kuwaiti oil executive around Tunis after he had received kidnap threats, and we both had watched over a wealthy Moroccan family with ties to a deposed leader when they were en route to new lives in Paris.

Karif Al-Fulan appeared in a couple of blog posts, but that was it. With him out of sight, it would be harder for anyone to carry out the death threats, and if all went well, Liam and I would be back in Tunis within a week, and Yaroush could set up a concert tour for Karif in the United States without fear.

I looked up from the computer with alarm when the front door opened. I hadn't heard anyone drive up or come to the gate. A short, elderly Arab woman smiled at me. "I am Alisa," she said in Arabic. "I clean house."

Of course she had a key, if her husband was the villa's caretaker. I welcomed her but said in fractured Arabic that a boy was still sleeping upstairs and could she be quiet.

She nodded and began in the kitchen. She'd finished most of the first floor when Karif, still naked, appeared at the top of the stairs, scratching his crotch. He saw the old woman, who looked up at him and smiled, and he jumped back toward the bedroom.

He reappeared a few minutes later wearing a skimpy bikini. "I'm going for a swim," he said.

I offered him breakfast, but he declined. "Mind if I keep you company out there?" I asked. "So I can get out of Alisa's way?"

He shrugged. I put on a pair of swim trunks, then joined Karif at the pool as he swam laps. I dragged one of the lounge chairs from the shade of the olive trees by the side of the house and opened it up. I sprayed on some suntan lotion, closed my eyes, and let the sun warm me. In the distance I could hear the sound of the surf and the motor of an occasional car on the ocean road.

When Karif climbed out of the pool and sat next to me, he said, "You think I am child."

I sat up and looked at him. "No, I think you're a man. But you're a man in a difficult situation. I know I act badly sometimes when I'm under pressure."

"Pressure," Karif said, nodding. "Pressure to sell records. Sing well. Make money so I never sing in street."

"It must be hard on you."

"I love to sing." He shook the water out of his hair, and a few drops splashed on my skin. The cool water felt great. "I am lucky for having talent."

Behind us, in the house, I heard the sound of the vacuum cleaner. "Would you like some lemonade?"

He smiled. "Yes, please."

When I returned with two tumblers, Karif was stretched out on his back on the lounge next to mine, his slender, half-erect cock pressed against the skimpy fabric. He looked up and smiled when I handed him the glass.

"You are very sexy man," he said as our fingers touched. "Different from Liam. He is being handsome, but you are having much passion."

"Thank you." I smiled and sat back on my own chair. He was a little slut, this kid, this twenty-five-year-old with doe eyes, a stiffening cock, and a hairless, shimmering expanse of latte-colored flesh. Against my better judgment, my own dick came to attention, and I was sure Karif noticed as I adjusted myself.

I loved Liam with all my heart, but I still got turned on by other guys, so I assumed he did too. I wasn't proud of being a horndog, but I'd spent so long in a loveless, sexless relationship before meeting Liam that I had years of repressed desire, which came out sometimes despite my active sex life with Liam.

I'd bounced right from my ex, Blake, to Liam's arms. I'd had my share of quick encounters when I was young, sowing wild oats. So had Liam. And I'd seen him get hard when we saw cute guys in bikinis on the beach at Hammamet or in the occasional Internet post.

Karif's hand strayed to his bathing suit. "When will the old woman leave?" he asked. His index finger traced lightly up his shaft. "Can you tell her to go now?"

Oh, Jesus. What was I doing, tempting our client in just the way I'd accused Liam of doing earlier that day? He was right; this was a very tricky assignment, and there was a fine line between being nice enough to Karif that he felt comfortable with us but not overstepping our professional bounds.

"You are very handsome and sexy," I said, sitting up and folding a towel over my crotch. "But you know that Liam and I are committed to each other. You're our client, and we're here to protect you. That's it."

Karif pouted again, though his dick still pressed against the skimpy fabric of his bikini.

Time to shift the conversation. "You're so talented. I loved your CD last night. Did you take singing lessons?"

"Only my mother." He sat back on his lounge. "She sing to me when I am boy. Then we sing together. She have very good ear, though I do not know it. She correct me, say if I listen and work hard I can be great singer." He sighed. "When I have twelve years, she catch fever. She die two days later."

"I'm so sorry. My mother died when I was in college."

"It was a great sadness." Karif looked away toward the barren land behind the villa. "I go live with my uncle and family, in Tunis. They have little house only, but they make corner for sleep. I am singing on street, for tourists."

The sun got too hot for me, and I shifted the position of the lounge chair into the shade. Karif, though, remained in the sun.

"How did you meet Yaroush?" I asked.

"In Beirut, he come to see me sing in club and say he will help me become big star."

"And now you are."

He closed his eyes, and soon he was asleep. He was a jumble of talent, fear, and hormones, and it was going to be a lot of work to keep him out of trouble.

Karif awoke as Liam pulled the Land Rover back into the driveway. "Good, you are back," Karif said when Liam came out to join us by the pool. "I would like to go out. Please? I will go crazy to stay here."

"All right," Liam said. "Where would you like to go?"

He shrugged. "Anywhere."

"Why don't we do a little sightseeing and find a place for lunch?" I suggested.

Karif agreed, so we all showered and changed quickly, then hopped into the Land Rover. "We should stay away from Houmt Souk, at least for a while," Liam said as he backed down the drive. "Too many people, too many tourists. We'll drive around and see the island instead."

We drove inland on a two-lane, tree-lined road past whitewashed houses with domed roofs and bright blue wrought-iron decor nestled beneath palms and olive trees. The cloudless blue sky lightened our mood, and by the time we reached the small town of Er Riadh, we were laughing and joking.

We stopped for lunch at a tourist café and sat at a corner table, with Karif between us. The waitress thought Liam and I were tourists, Karif our guide, and addressed all the choices to him. He played the role well, explaining the dishes to us in effusive and sometimes inaccurate English.

For the first time since we met him at the Hotel Africa, he looked like he was having fun, putting aside the threats he had received. It felt good, knowing we could have this effect on him while still protecting him. Maybe we'd be adding therapy to the services we offered.

The waitress asked Karif if he was taking us to see the synagogue of Er Riadh. "Is oldest temple in north of Africa," she said proudly in heavily accented English.

"Perhaps," he said to her. "If my clients wish." He made a show of paying the café bill. As we pulled away in the Land Rover, he said, "I would like to visit the synagogue, if you will go."

I'd read about the synagogue; it had what was possibly the world's oldest Torah. It had been bombed in 1992, killing nineteen people. I looked at Liam, who shrugged, and we followed signs through the town to the synagogue.

"My mother say my father was Jew," Karif said as we walked through the whitewashed stucco gate surmounted by seven nearly round arches. They reminded me of the traditional candelabra at my family's synagogue back in New Jersey.

"Really?" I asked. "I am Jewish myself."

"Yes, I see you have *tahara*," Karif said.

I didn't understand the word, but Liam did. He made scissoring motions with his fingers. Oh, circumcised. Even though it had happened to me years before, when I was only eight days old, my body still recoiled at the idea.

"I also," Karif said. He looked to Liam. "But you are not?"

"My father thought it was a barbaric custom," Liam said. "Even though most boys in the US get circumcised in the hospital, he refused to let them touch me."

"I am with men who are tahara and men who are not," Karif said. "I prefer the men who are not."

I moved closer to Liam but smiled at Karif. Read the body language, boy. This man is taken, and his uncircumcised dick is mine to enjoy, not yours.

Liam understood me and smiled slyly. Karif ignored us both and walked into the synagogue, where the bright blue color we had seen on the exterior of many houses was repeated in elaborate arches and tiled walls. A clerestory of windows, surmounted by red and green fanlights, filled the room with light. There were elaborate details everywhere I looked, from the rococo chandelier to the balcony railings. The whole place was a sensory orgy.

As we wandered the room, I asked Karif, "Did you know your father?"

He shook his head. "I do not know if he marry my mother. He leave soon after I am born."

We stopped in front of the ancient Torah scroll, propped open in a wooden case with a sky-blue cloth over it. "So old," Karif said. "The people who made this lived so long ago."

"And they had the same troubles we have today," I said. "That, at least, doesn't change."

"I guess you are being right," Karif said thoughtfully

8 – DANCE FLOOR

We left the synagogue and continued south toward Guellala, where Liam turned to head back around the island. We stopped in Aghir for dinner at a luxury hotel, Liam leaving me and Karif in the lobby for a few minutes while he walked around the property and spoke to the mâitre d' in the restaurant.

While we waited, Karif and I ordered cocktails at the bar. It was a spacious room with easy exit to the lobby. The walls were mirrored, and racks of tiny lights hung from the ceiling. Scattered couples and groups sat at tables around the large dance floor, and six British women in their twenties giggled and drank at the far end of the bar from us. It looked like a safe place, and I tipped the bartender well in case we wanted to stop back later for a nightcap.

When Liam returned, we walked to a restaurant overlooking the kidney-shaped pool, nearly empty now that evening was falling. Spotlights illuminated the blue-green water dotted with a few inflatable floats. A swim-up bar at the far end was already closed, and a scattering of beach towels rested on lounge chairs.

The mâitre d' welcomed Karif by name, said something nice about his latest CD, and led us to a table backed against the stucco wall, with the rest of the tables laid out before us. The pool was ringed with two-story buildings, but the position of our table meant no one from a balcony could see us -- or draw a bead on Karif with a high-powered rifle.

When your client wants to dine out, the best thing to do is to make arrangements in advance -- minimize wait time, secure a table with easy access to the exit in case of emergency, and so on. Baksheesh, which oils the functioning of the Arab world, comes in handy. I was sure that Liam had promised the maître d' a big tip, perhaps even return business once the fatwa had been lifted and Karif could publicize where he vacationed.

It was a magical setting as night fell and the stars came out. Tiny white lights twinkled at the bases of palm trees, and the slight breeze made their fronds dance. The swirling rhythms of Tunisian music played softly in the background, and the air was full of delicious scents from other diners' dishes.

I couldn't help wishing Liam and I had been there alone, without the distraction of Karif. Liam ordered us a bottle of the Vieux Magon he and I drank the first time we met. It was a rich, ruby red wine with notes of cherry and lemon, and Karif toasted us. "Thank you for looking after me," he said. "I know I am not always nicest client."

We tipped our glasses together, then ordered platters of grilled lamb and couscous. Liam and I were careful to make sure that Karif drank more wine than we did, constantly peppering him with questions about the places he had sung, asking about how fans had treated him in the past.

It was useful information. Our primary objective was to protect Karif from any death threats but managing a celebrity's fans could be an important part of a bodyguard's job. Was he accustomed to being besieged for autographs? Did his female fans crowd around hoping for kisses or hugs or a chance to touch him?

"I love my fans," he said. "I am not big star yet. When I am at concert, there are askings for autographs afterward. Sometimes ladies will kiss."

"And when you are not at a concert?" Liam asked. "Do they recognize you on the street?"

"Not so much. I have only two CDs so far. But I want be big star someday, like Bono or Madonna."

The food was good, and the wine was working on Karif; he was relaxed and happy. "I would like go back to bar, please," he said when the waitress had cleared away the dishes. "For dancing. Very nice dance floor there."

"We'll look in," Liam said.

Karif strode into the bar and tried to sit at a table by the edge of the dance floor. Liam shook his head and nodded toward the wall. Karif frowned but followed us to a more secure table. He ordered a double whiskey from the barmaid, while Liam ordered club soda and I had a virgin piña colada.

The bar wasn't that crowded -- just us, a group of young German men on holiday, and a scattering of other tourist couples. The British women had moved on, and there was a low energy level in the room. Two couples slow danced to "The Sea of Love" by The Honeydrippers under a spinning disco ball.

Then the song changed to "YMCA" by the Village People, and all the German men streamed out onto the floor and started dancing like mad. Karif jumped up to join them. I looked at Liam. "We could sit here and watch," I said. "Or we could watch him just as closely from the dance floor."

He frowned. I realized we'd never danced together before, at least not in public. "Come on, Liam. You told me yourself that the bodyguard has to join in the activities of the client."

Karif plunged into the middle of the group of German men, while Liam and I stayed to the side of the dance floor. I guess dance lessons weren't part of Liam's SEAL training, because his movements were stiff and distracted. "Come on, loosen up," I said, poking him as I swayed my hips and shook my arms. "It's not supposed to be painful."

He cracked a smile, and within a verse or two he was relaxing, moving in time to the music, even joining in the arm movements to the *Y*, the *M*, the *C*, and the *A*.

When the next song, Ritchie Valens singing "La Bamba" came on, Karif remained with the Germans, and Liam took my hands and began swaying his hips in a Latin move I didn't know he had. Just the feeling of his hands in mine was a turn-on, even if I hadn't noticed the boner pressing against the front of his khaki shorts. He pulled me close to him, then pushed me away, his body moving with the same sure grace he demonstrated slipping through a crowd or moving around our house.

When he pulled me back to him again, our bodies connected, and he slipped his hands out of mine and around my back, holding me close to him. My body felt loose, double-jointed, as I followed his steps. I loved to dance; back in college a female friend and I had won a dance contest sponsored by the student government. My ex, Blake, wasn't a dancer, so I was out of practice, but just like riding a bike or sucking a dick, it came back to me.

Karif was still dancing with the Germans. I couldn't tell if they were gay or just on an all-male vacation. For all I knew, they were insurance agents attending an international conference. Karif looked happy among them, dancing with one, then another, then a third.

The music shifted to a Latin song I didn't know, but it didn't matter to Liam; we kept dancing. He backed away a bit, shifted his body, and put his left leg between mine, pulling me to him. My dick was up against his thigh, his dick against mine, and I nearly swooned from the ecstasy of it.

He bent his head down and nuzzled my neck. I said, "I'm going to come in my shorts if you don't stop that."

"Maybe I want you to come in your shorts."

"Really?" I leaned back. "Not in your mouth or in your ass?"

He laughed. "You've got a point." He grabbed my hands and swung me out and around, then let me go and began doing the twist. We played around, trying all the sixties and seventies dances we remembered -- the bump, the hustle, the swim.

I could tell he was keeping an eye on Karif as much as I was. Our client returned to the table just long enough to grab his whiskey and down it, then went back to his German friends. As we watched, he zeroed in on one beefy blond with a mustache and a black T-shirt that clung seductively to his muscular chest. His pants were so tight I could tell he was semihard. Either that or he had a monster dick.

Karif moved in closer to the German until he was dirty dancing with the man, rubbing his ass up against the German's crotch. No matter how the man moved back, Karif was on him. Finally the man pushed Karif away.

Liam tensed up as Karif began shouting something. He swung at the German, and Liam let me go and turned toward them. By the time he reached Karif, the Germans had clustered around their friend. *"Bitte, bitte,"* Liam said, holding his hands up, palms out. He strong-armed Karif and dragged him out of the bar. The Germans clustered together as if they wanted to follow, and I was left facing them down, my arms crossed.

I didn't speak German, but I got the gist of what they were saying. Karif had miscalculated, taking European friendliness to mean sexual availability, and they wanted to show him the error of his ways.

Fortunately the DJ saw what was going on and switched songs to a happy German drinking song, and they turned back, linking arms and singing along. I hustled over and dropped some dinars on the bar, motioning that I wanted to buy a round for the crowd.

When the Germans began their second verse, I slipped away and followed Liam and Karif outside.

9 – HAVING MORALS

By the time I reached the parking lot, Liam had Karif backed against the Land Rover. "You can't do that. I have enough trouble protecting you from whoever wants to kill you. I wasn't hired to drag you out of barroom brawls."

Karif crossed his arms and stared at Liam. "I am wanting to dance with men. They should not have danced with me if they did not want."

"You shoved your ass at that man like a stripper doing a lap dance," Liam said. "He showed you he wasn't interested, but you wouldn't let up."

Karif said nothing, just stared to the side. Liam shrugged. "Fine. Get in the car."

Instead of taking his usual front seat next to Liam, Karif climbed into the backseat and reclined, making it clear he didn't want me with him. I got in the front with Liam, resisting making any comment about his behavior with the client.

Traffic was heavy even that late, and I worried that every time Liam came to a stop Karif might jump out of the car and run off toward one of the hotels or condos. I leaned close to Liam and whispered, "This car have childproof locks?"

Liam raised his eyebrows, but at the next light he peered down at the controls on his door and flipped a switch. I wanted to lighten the atmosphere in the car, but I couldn't think of anything to say that didn't sound stupid. So I kept quiet. We drove back to the Villa Palma, taking the coast road all the way around the Zone Touristique.

When we walked in the house, Karif stalked away, then climbed the stairs to the second floor two at a time. When he reached his room, he slammed the door behind him.

"Weren't you the one who told me not to get angry at the client?" I asked.

"I wasn't angry. I was just clear about Karif's obligations."

"Oh. Do a lot of jobs end up like this?" I asked, pulling a bottle of water from the refrigerator. We'd both had enough wine for the night. Even though we were back at the villa, it was important that we didn't let down our guard. "Babysitting? Because I have to say, I'm not loving this."

Liam found a couple of glasses in the cabinet and held them out as I poured. "You do what you have to do. He's a client."

I carried my glass into the living room, where I sat on the overstuffed couch. Liam came in behind me, then flopped down next to me, turning sideways so his feet were in my lap. He handed me a tube of foot cream. "As long as you're in the right position."

I laughed and took the cream from him. "When I first came out, I was like a kid in a candy store," I said as I uncapped the cream and squeezed some into my palm. "I'd go to a gay bar, and I'd feel like I could sleep with any man in the room if I wanted."

"Cocky attitude." Liam smiled and lifted his glass to mine.

I began massaging his right foot. "I was young and cute, and yeah, I was cocky. Like Karif."

"Not quite, I'm sure. I'll bet you were quite the sexy boy when you were younger," Liam said as I rubbed my thumb over the ball of his foot.

"And I'm not now?"

"You're quite the sexy man now," Liam said.

"Good answer. But then you always know just the right thing to say." I squeezed out some more cream and began massaging his toes. "But it's frustrating, you know? You hold back on those desires, for whatever reasons, and then once you let go, you want to get laid. To be locked up with us must be tough for him."

"I know. I went through the same thing myself. But it's more than that. You take a kid like Karif, who's never had anything, and suddenly he's a big star, with lots of money, two platinum albums, and a record company to spoil him. He has to learn to balance that freedom."

"Too bad one of us can't just fuck him," I said, trying to sound innocent but keeping an eye on Liam. Even at his pouty worst, Karif was very handsome. Some men would swoon for those dark doe eyes, the artfully arranged curls of black hair, the boyish enthusiasm. But would Liam?

Liam turned to look at me. "Excuse me? Are you saying you want to fuck the client?"

"No. I know that's against the rules. He's horny and he needs to get laid. But we can't let him pick up random guys in a bar."

I was relieved Liam hadn't disagreed with me, hadn't considered the idea of having sex with Karif. I switched to his other foot and kept rubbing.

"You're such a romantic most of the time, Aidan. And then sometimes it seems like sex is just a transaction with you."

I shrugged. "Isn't there a difference between sex and love?"

"Not to me. I wouldn't want to have sex with you if I didn't love you."

"Come on, Liam." I pulled back from his feet, capped the cream, and tossed it to the coffee table. "You never had sex with a guy just for fun? Or because you'd led him on in some bar and then felt like you had to go through with it?"

I hadn't realized the conversation was going to go where it had and didn't like the way Liam looked at me.

"Is that what you do?"

I was determined to tell the truth, because I wasn't going to let any little lies come between Liam and me. So I took a deep breath and said, "I did. Until I met Blake. He was into monogamy, and I didn't want to rock the boat." I had lived with Blake Chennault, a successful patent attorney, for eleven years in Philadelphia until he'd kicked me to the curb, leading to my arrival in Tunis and my meeting with Liam.

I reached out to put a hand on Liam's thigh. "Does that bother you?" I asked. "I never pretended to be a virgin. I fucked a lot of guys before Blake. But I loved him, and I love you. I won't go out looking for another guy as long as I have you."

"Then you shouldn't be so jealous every time Karif, or any other guy, looks at me," Liam said. "You know how I feel about you, that I'm just as committed to you as you are to me. I don't like it when you go all drama queen on me. It's like you're saying you don't trust me."

"I do trust you." Looking at it from his point of view, I realized he could think I didn't believe him when he said monogamy was important to him too. "I'm sorry if I ever made it seem like I didn't."

Liam didn't say anything for a while. "I love the way you plunge into things. But sometimes you let your enthusiasm get ahead of your brain. You do understand that sex with the client is never part of the job, don't you?"

Sex was indeed one of the many pitfalls I'd been warned about in bodyguard school. We weren't to supply illegal drugs to our client, procure prostitutes, or get personally involved. The key to our success was our professionalism. As soon as the client saw us as friends, sex objects, or underlings who could be pushed around, our effectiveness was compromised.

Of course, most of the discussions about sex during my weeklong program had been of the heterosexual variety. Male agents were warned against getting too close to the wives they were protecting; female agents were cautioned against wearing revealing clothing, even on assignments that involved nightlife, to keep male clients from coming on to them.

They'd touched on gay clients briefly -- mostly because so many of my classmates were big, macho guys with bursting muscles, and the staff wanted to make sure they understood gay clients had to be handled with the same respect as straight ones. I had never mentioned the fact that Liam and I were lovers, and as far as I knew, I'd passed for straight among my classmates.

I knew it was wrong, and I was just irritating Liam by talking about sex with Karif, but I couldn't help it. Karif was very cute, and though I didn't want to sleep with him myself, I wanted to be damn sure that Liam didn't either. "Don't be such a prude, Liam."

"There's a difference between being a prude and having morals," he said, turning so he was sitting next to me on the sofa. "The client's paying you to do a job. If you add sex to that job description, you're nothing more than a hooker."

That stung. I'd never considered who was actually paying us, though chances were even if the record company was writing the check, they were taking it out of money they owed Karif. I imagined Karif tossing a few bills on the bed after Liam or I had sucked his cock or fucked his ass -- and how dirty that would make us both feel.

Liam must have seen something in my eyes, because he softened his tone. "If you're not going to be a moral person, you can't be a good bodyguard. Protecting someone is a duty, and you have to embrace all sides of that responsibility. Sometimes it's your job to protect the client from his own bad impulses. Even if part of you thinks his impulses aren't that bad."

Something inside me finally released. I believed Liam and had faith that even if Karif kept coming on to him, he'd keep refusing.

I leaned up and kissed him. He bore down on me, the pressure of his lips on mine making my body tingle. He gnawed on my lower lip, and my head dropped back against the sofa as my heart rate accelerated and my dick stiffened.

He began unbuttoning my shirt, his rough hands going beneath the fabric and cupping the two round globes surrounding my nipples. Then his head was there, his mouth taking one nipple at a time, laving it with his tongue, then gently nibbling with his teeth.

It was the kind of attention that made me crazy, turned me into nothing more than a quivering mass of flesh that wanted sex from him as soon as possible. I leaned back against the cushions, which sank under my weight, and ran my hands through Liam's short blondish-brown hair. I wanted to push his head down to my dick, but I knew he'd resist. We had to take sex at his pace, slow and sensual. I felt like an odalisque, sprawled out on the sofa with desire wafting out of me.

I slipped my shirt off my shoulders, exposing my chest to him. I'd always been in good shape, but life with Liam, including a regular regimen of workouts followed by athletic sex, had tightened my abs and was pumping my biceps in tiny increments. I would never have the kind of muscular, Greek-god figure he had, but sometimes when I was alone in our bedroom back in Tunis, I'd lie on the bed naked, caressing my body and imagining myself as a porn-magazine centerfold.

Liam licked his way down my chest and tickled my belly button with his tongue. The sensation gave me goose bumps, as if he was finding a new way to penetrate me. I couldn't help it; I pushed his head down toward my crotch.

He resisted, but he ran his hand up against the fabric covering my stiff dick. My body shook with excitement as he picked at my belt, then my zipper. He pushed my shorts down, leaving my boxers in place, and lifted my ass off the sofa so that he could discard my outerwear.

Liam preferred me naked, or nearly so, while he remained fully clothed. He liked to make love to me, licking and sucking and turning me into his sex slave, while remaining in control. If I was very good, he'd open his pants and let me suck him, or even better, prop my legs up over his shoulders and stick his cock up my ass. But quite often he'd just blow me or jerk me off, then back away.

As I lay back on the sofa, he pulled my dick out of the slit of my boxers and swiped his tongue along the length of it. "Oh, God," I whispered, my voice shaking. I arched my neck, closed my eyes, and focused on the sensation of warmth and moisture as he swallowed my dick. Shutting out the visuals like that made me more sensitive to his touch and the sound of his mouth going up and down on me.

I heard a sound in the background -- was it a footstep? The creak of the wooden floor? I was so caught up in the sensation of Liam's mouth on my dick that I ignored it.

He took me all the way down his throat so that his nose was slammed up against my pubic hair, then backed off, suctioning me like a vacuum. He grabbed my ass so that his right fingers were poised at my crack, and his index finger found my hole and penetrated me.

I arched my back and pressed my ass up off the sofa, impaling myself farther on his finger and pressing my dick deeper down his throat. My body felt like it was on fire; I was sweating, and my heart was beating so fast I was afraid it would jump out of my chest.

Liam stuck a second finger up my ass as he continued to suck me. I started whimpering, my body twitching in tiny spasms. I began to buck forward against his mouth. Then I heard that sound again.

Had Karif come out of the bedroom? Was he watching us? We should have gone into our bedroom and closed the door, but I'd been so caught up in the moment as Liam began to make love to me on the sofa that getting up was the last thing on my mind.

Liam quickened his pace, and I pushed forward against his mouth, and if Karif was watching us, I didn't care. We'd put on a show for the little bastard. This was me, having sex with my man. Get over it and move on.

Liam dug his index finger even deeper in my ass, until I could feel it jabbing my prostate. I thrashed my head back and forth against the sofa pillow. I wanted to come so badly, but my body was taking its time. I squeezed my ass cheeks around Liam's fingers and savored his hot, moist breath around my dick.

And then it started. My breathing quickened, I got light-headed, and electric sensations swept through my body. I felt like I was holding my breath, as if my whole body was poised on the threshold of something amazing. Then, whimpering, I came in Liam's mouth, and every thought in my head was swept away.

10 – DISAPPEARING ACT

The next morning Karif came downstairs as I was fixing bacon and eggs for Liam and myself. I prepared a plate for him too and took it out to the dining room, where he sat at the table reading a copy of the *International Herald Tribune* I had picked up at the hotel the night before. When I put the dish down, I noticed he was poring over an article on Palestinian politics.

When he was finished with the article, he pushed the paper aside. "Will we be able to go out again today?"

"Will you behave?" Liam asked. "My job is to keep you safe. If you cooperate with us, we'll go out. If you don't, we'll stay here."

Karif lowered his gaze to the table. "I'm sorry. I had too much drink last night, and I behaved badly." He looked up at Liam, smiling. "Will you forgive me?"

"I'll talk to Yaroush," Liam said. "If there have been no more threats, then yes, we can go out. Where would you like to go?"

"I want to go into Houmt Souk. I would like to go shopping."

Liam looked at me. "That's your department," he said. Liam was a typical male when it came to shopping; he liked to walk into a store, identify what he needed, buy it, and get out. I, on the other hand, loved the experience of shopping -- picking things up, evaluating them, imagining them in my life.

"The food was very good," Karif said, leaning back in his chair. "If it would be all right with you, I would like to use your laptop."

I looked at Liam. "Sure," he said.

Liam went outside to do some stretching exercises, and I cleaned up while Karif did whatever it was he wanted online. When he returned the laptop to me and went upstairs, I looked at the search history, assuming he'd been looking for information on himself. Instead all the sites focused on the political situation in Palestine I'd seen mentioned in the newspaper.

"Look at this," I said, calling Liam over when he came back inside. "What do you think he's up to?"

He pulled on his reading glasses and scanned through the sites himself. When he finished, he looked at me and shrugged. "He's not Palestinian. Maybe Yaroush will know what he's looking for."

Liam went out to check the wall that ran around the property and look over the access roads to the villa, and I did push-ups and sit-ups until my muscles felt like jelly. When Karif came downstairs, he was naked. "I would like to swim," he said.

"Would you like me to join you?"

"If you wish."

I was only wearing a pair of loose shorts, and for a moment I thought of using them as a swimsuit, but that would be prissy and old-maidish since Karif was naked. And after all, Liam had been naked with him and justified it to me. I should be able to do the same thing. I grabbed some towels and left them -- and my shorts -- on the lounge chair. I stepped into the cool water, taking my time, as Karif began to swim laps.

Liam went back inside as Karif and I were swimming, and I saw him pull the laptop to himself at the kitchen table and put on a headset. I assumed that meant he was calling Yaroush in Rome using Voice over IP software. He came out to the pool when he finished, shucked his shorts, and dived naked into the deep end. There wasn't room for the three of us to swim, so I got out and stretched on a lounge chair. The sun's heat dried my skin quickly as Liam and Karif swam.

"Would you like to go into Houmt Souk for lunch?" Liam asked Karif when they got out of the pool.

Karif beamed. "Yes, that would be very nice."

We showered and dressed, and as we were leaving, Alisa came in to clean. Liam spoke to her in Arabic, warning her not to let anyone in while we were gone, and then we drove down the ocean road into Houmt Souk. The buildings were similar to those we'd seen elsewhere on the island, white-washed stucco ornamented with turquoise window frames. Many of the buildings were surmounted by small white domes.

We navigated the narrow streets of the town in search of a parking space. "I want to go into that shop," Karif demanded, pointing to a store with a display of gold and silver jewelry in the window.

"As soon as we park," Liam said. "We'll come back here."

"No. You let Aidan and me off here and then come." He turned to me. "You protect me, yes, Aidan?"

"Fine," Liam said. He pulled to the curb. "Keep your radio on, Aidan. I'll be back in a few minutes."

The air was hot after the cool of the car, and I was glad to hurry into the store, which was heavily air-conditioned. Karif and I browsed a display of men's jewelry in gold. He picked out a necklace of finely wrought gold links and put it around his neck. I admired the way it rested against his sleek, bronzed throat. "It's beautiful," I said as he looked at himself in the mirror.

"You try one too," he said.

I resisted, but the shopkeeper held an identical chain out to me, and I bowed my neck so he could slip it on. It was as light as water, and the gold glistened through the dark hair at the top of my chest. "I take three," Karif told the shopkeeper in Arabic. "One for each of us," he said to me.

"Oh no," I said. "We couldn't accept --"

"I insist." He smiled. "Please? Is apology for behavior last night."

Before I could argue further, the shopkeeper put a third chain in a silk bag, and Karif handed him a gold American Express card. Karif scrawled a signature on the receipt, which the shopkeeper put together with two more silk bags, one each for the chains Karif and I wore. He was shoveling it all in a paper shopping bag when Karif said, "I'll be outside."

"Karif, wait," I said, but he ducked out the door. By the time I got out to the street, he was gone. I darted into the shop next door. No Karif. Then back out to the street and to the store on the other side. I pulled out the radio and called Liam. "Where are you?" I asked.

"About a block away. What's up?"

"Karif gave me the slip, the little bastard." I saw Liam approaching and hurried down the street to meet him.

One thing I loved about Liam was that when something went wrong, he skipped the recrimination stage and went directly to action. "You take that side of the street, I'll take this one," he said. "Go to the end of the block, and if you don't find him, come back here. Keep the radio on."

I went in and out of every store on the block, asking for Karif. "I'm sorry," I said, when I met Liam back in front of the jeweler's. "I tried to stop him, but…"

"You didn't know he was going to run." Liam grimaced. "I should have anticipated that. He was too nice this morning."

"What's he playing at? He's acting like a child."

"Yes, he's been acting that way since we met him. He's too headstrong, and he's not mature enough to understand the danger he's in."

We stood under the awning of a store selling woven blankets in shades of reds, blues, and browns. "You have a map of the town in your guidebook?" Liam asked. We were on the Avenue Habib Bourguiba; he was the first president of the Tunisian republic, and it seemed like every town in Tunisia had a street named after him. The port was to our left, a warren of souks straight ahead.

I handed Liam the map and asked, "Where do you think he'll go?"

He shrugged. "I don't think he wants to leave the island. He's just messing with us, trying to assert his independence. My guess is that he's wandering around the souks."

We split up, planning a methodical search of the market, ending at the Place Hedi Chaker on the other side. "Don't yell at him," Liam said. "He'll just run away again. Radio me, play it cool, and maneuver him toward the meeting place."

"Will do." I veered right, passing leather markets, more jewelry stores, and a display of beautiful pottery. I was cranky that I couldn't enjoy myself and angry that I'd let Karif fool me and show how inept I was as a bodyguard.

I prowled in and out of souks, resisting the pleas of the shopkeepers. Twice I saw a man I thought was Karif and rushed forward, only to realize I'd been mistaken. The heat bore down on me, and I stopped to buy a bottle of water. I looked for a dark place to lean back and drink -- and that's when I spotted Karif.

He was on his knees, his mouth at the crotch of a dirty-looking young guy with brown dreadlocks who leaned back against one of the ubiquitous robin's egg blue doorways. A broken couscous pot, its pointed spout still intact, rested next to them, near a pile of what looked like someone's old clothes.

I stepped back, keeping them in sight, and tried to raise Liam on the radio. No answer. He was out of range, or there was something in the souk that interfered with reception. So I was on my own.

Liam had said not to confront Karif, but I was so angry, and worried that a cop might stumble into the alley, that I couldn't help myself. I marched up and grabbed him. "Are you crazy!" I said, pulling his shoulder. "You could get arrested, thrown in jail. Your career could go down the tubes!"

I positioned myself so that no one passing the alley could see them, then said, "Get the fuck up!" Karif fell back to the pavement, leaving the guy's stiff dick sticking out of his shorts, glistening with saliva and precome.

"What the fuck?" the dreadlock guy said with a thick British accent.

"Yeah, my thoughts exactly." I pulled a couple of hundred-dinar notes from my wallet and handed them to him. "Get lost."

He took the money and zipped up his shorts. "See ya, mate," he said. He turned and ran from the alley.

"I am staying Villa Palma, Mezraia," Karif called as the dirty guy disappeared around the corner. Then he turned to me. "You act like you are my father!" he said, getting to his feet and wiping a hand across his mouth. "I do what I like. Is not your business!"

"I'm not your father," I said. "But it is my business. I'm in charge of your safety. And that includes keeping you out of jail."

I was so angry I was shaking. I could imagine what would have happened if the police had discovered Karif. The scandal, Liam and me being fired, Liam reconsidering the wisdom of letting me be his junior partner. And then our relationship dissolving, leaving me to return to the States, no love, no job. And all because this stupid slut couldn't control himself.

My arm remained locked on his as I dragged him to the Place Hedi Chaker. My chest was drenched with sweat, and I snarled at any shopkeeper who tried to approach us. I tried to calm down, struggling to remember what I had learned in bodyguard school, but it was no use.

"I bought you necklace!" Karif said as we walked. "You must be nice to me."

"I don't need your fucking necklace," I said, feeling it burn around my neck. I would have pulled it off and thrown it to the ground, but I didn't want to let go of Karif.

Liam came striding toward us a block before we reached the square. "Let him go, Aidan," he said. "What did I tell you?"

"See?" Karif said as I released his arm. He rubbed the place I had been gripping him for effect. "Liam treat me nice."

"Liam doesn't know what you were doing." I wiped a hand across my forehead and flapped my shirt against my skin. Nothing worked to cool me down. I was even angrier that Liam had been rough with Karif the night before and it had been all right for him then.

"We'll talk about it back at the villa." Liam put his arm around Karif's shoulders and turned him ninety degrees.

"I want to shop more!" Karif tried to shift away, but I could see Liam exerting a gentle pressure on our client's shoulders.

"Nope," Liam said. "Not today." He led the way down the crowded sidewalk, smiling and shaking his head to the shopkeepers. Karif kept on arguing, but neither of us answered him. The sun blazed down on us as we emerged from the narrow streets, and Karif stopped complaining.

A taxi turned the corner too sharply, coming so close that I banged a hand on its hood. Liam turned back to me, his eyes flashing, looking for any excuse to lash out at me because of the way I'd dealt with Karif. I set my lips in a grim line and challenged him to complain. By the time we reached the Land Rover, we were each locked in our own anger

11 – UNEXPECTED VISITOR

Once again Karif stomped out of the Land Rover as soon as we got to the house and retreated to his bedroom. "Did you not listen to me when I told you to be nice to him?" Liam asked as we walked inside.

"I didn't do anything more than you did last night. And besides, he was giving a blowjob to a stranger," I said. "On his knees, in an alley just off one of the main streets. Anybody could have seen him."

Liam shook his head. "This kid is a loose cannon. Yaroush said there haven't been new threats. I'm thinking we take him back Tunis tomorrow and call this assignment done."

"Sounds great to me."

Karif didn't come downstairs for dinner, so Liam and I ate together out by the pool. We didn't talk much; I was still too angry at Karif, irritated at Liam, and scared about what might have happened. I couldn't tell what Liam was thinking.

The house phone rang as I was cleaning up, and Liam answered. I couldn't hear his end of the conversation, but when he came into the kitchen, his face was stormy. "We're not getting out of this so easily," he said. "The record company got another threat this afternoon. Whoever is after Karif knows we're on Djerba. The threat to kill him was very specific."

"Shit."

"My feelings exactly. I'm going to go up and check on him.

Make sure he hasn't slithered out a window and run off. Maybe I can convince him to behave."

I had glasses of Vieux Magon ready when Liam came back downstairs. "Any luck?" I asked.

He shook his head. "He doesn't seem to care."

We took the wine out to the patio and sat there in the growing dusk, not saying anything. I thought about how much this new life mattered to me -- this love, this work, even this heat-stroked country. How I didn't want to give any of it up.

Liam and I both heard the noise at the same time. A *thud*, something heavy hitting the ground. And then a second *thud*, a minute or two later, accompanied by a grunt of pain. Liam pointed up toward Karif's room, and though I didn't want to leave my partner alone to face whoever was out there, I knew our responsibility was to protect the client.

As quietly as I could, I slid open the glass door and slipped inside, then hurried upstairs. I pulled one of the two GLOCKs out of the bedside drawer and grabbed a high-powered flashlight. Then I burst into Karif's room without knocking. He was lying on the bed, naked, his hand wrapped around his dick.

"Put some shorts on," I said, throwing a pair at him. "There's an intruder on the grounds. Liam is going after him."

Karif sat paralyzed on the bed, staring at me. At least he stopped jerking himself. "Come on," I said. "I want to get back down there in case he needs backup."

"You think it is someone to kill me?"

"Don't know. Come on."

He pulled on the shorts and followed me downstairs. "Stay there," I said, pointing at the bottom step. "If anything happens, run back up to your room and lock the door."

He looked scared shitless. I heard a yell from the backyard and rushed over to the patio door. Looking out, I saw Liam with a man in a choke hold. I turned the flashlight on them.

"Motherfucker," I said. "That's the guy Karif was blowing in the alley."

"I told you, mate," the guy said in that same lower-class British accent.

Liam let him go, and Karif appeared behind me. "Gavin!" Karif said. "You found me!"

"See? I told you, he invited me here. To finish what you interrupted."

"Come on," Liam said. "Let's go inside."

"Can I bring my duffle?"

"I'll get it." Liam pushed Gavin forward, and I stepped back to let him in the house.

Up close he looked just as dirty as he had in the souk, and I wondered what Karif had seen in him. He had a beefy chest and stocky legs, a wiry beard and shoulder-length light brown hair curled into filthy dreadlocks. His T-shirt and shorts were grimy, as were the leather sandals on his feet. I didn't want him sitting on any of the furniture.

Karif rushed over and hugged him. "I am so glad you came!"

Gavin embraced him, squeezing his butt. "Cute thing like you? How could I resist?"

Liam came inside carrying the duffle. "You. Sit," he said, pointing at Gavin. I was glad to see him settle on the floor with Karif. That meant we wouldn't have to fumigate any of the chairs. Liam hoisted Gavin's duffle on the dining room table and started emptying it.

"Oi! That's private, that," Gavin said.

"Shut it." Liam looked up long enough to glare, then went back to his work. He pulled out a purple passport with the British seal on it and flipped it open, looking from Gavin to the picture. "Name?"

"Gavin Jones."

"Address?" Gavin gave him a street address in London, which appeared to match what was in the passport, because Liam closed it and tossed it to the table. He went through the rest of the stuff: a lot of grotty clothes and a string of condoms encased in yellow plastic.

"Why are you here?" Liam said when he'd finished.

"Told you. Wanted to finish what Karif and me started in the souk."

I was an Anglophile at heart, watching endless episodes of *Masterpiece Theatre*, *EastEnders*, the British version of *Antiques Roadshow*, and almost everything else on BBC America, so I had a good feeling for accents. I thought he was from the north of England, maybe Birmingham or Yorkshire.

Liam came over and sat next to me on the sofa, facing Karif and Gavin, who were holding hands, their thighs touching. Young love, I thought. How sweet.

"What are we going to do with you?" Liam asked.

"I want him stay," Karif said. "He is my guest."

"And if he rolls over and stabs you in the middle of the night, it's our fault," Liam said.

"You've got a filthy mind," Gavin said. "Who thinks like that? Stab him, indeed."

"You know who he is?" Liam asked Gavin, nodding toward Karif.

"Told you. Karif. Chap who was blowing me in the souk."

"Yeah, yeah, I got that part," Liam said. "You know his last name? What he does for a living?"

Either Gavin didn't know, or he was an excellent liar. "Ain't got a clue."

Liam reached for the cover to Karif's second CD and tossed it to Gavin, who scanned it. "Cor," he said to Karif. "That's you?"

Karif blushed. "Yes."

"Sexy you are, and talented too," Gavin said. He kissed Karif on the cheek.

I leaned close to Liam and spoke quietly. "He could keep Karif out of trouble."

Liam stood up. "Aidan and I need to have a discussion." He looked at Gavin the way I'd seen him stare down bad guys before. "But we're just going to be in the kitchen, so don't even think of trying to pull something."

"There is no way we are letting that dirty weirdo stay in this house," Liam said when we were in the kitchen. "Who turns up like that in the middle of the night?"

"I think it's sweet," I said, leaning back against the counter. "Karif told him we were staying here, and Gavin tracked him down."

"Sweet, my ass," Liam said. "You don't know who this guy is or where he's from. What if he's a Muslim radical who's carrying out the fatwa? What if he's a trained assassin?"

I burst into laughter. "That goofy kid out there?" I asked. "A Muslim radical? An assassin? Are you on drugs?"

"Once again you're letting your dick get ahead of your brain," Liam said. "I saw the way you looked at him when he walked in the door. You think he's cute, so you don't believe he can be dangerous."

"Excuse me? You saw the way I looked at him? How exactly was that?"

"You looked at him like you wanted to fuck him," Liam said. He stood there with his hands on his hips.

"Uh, Liam? I'm supposed to be the jealous, dizzy queen in this relationship, not you." I leaned over and kissed him on the lips. "I don't want to fuck Gavin. I don't want to fuck Karif. You're the only man I want to have sex with, in this house or out of it."

He looked at me. "I believe you." His shoulders relaxed, and he smiled. "But that doesn't change the situation. We can't let a complete stranger move in with us while we're trying to protect our client."

"I'll do a database search on him, all right?" I said, opening the laptop. "If he comes up clean, can he stay?"

"We'll see." He turned and walked back into the living room, where I heard him ask for Gavin's passport again. He returned and handed it to me as I logged into a database we used for identity checks. I entered Gavin's name, birthdate, and passport number, and received confirmation that they matched information in the issuing government's records.

"His passport's legit," I said. Without going through a much more extensive check, I couldn't find out if he had a criminal record, but at least he wasn't on any of the government-issued watch lists for suspected terrorists.

"Is this good enough for you?" I asked Liam. "He's a horny guy who's got his eye on Karif, and the feeling seems to be mutual. If he's got Gavin, Karif is unlikely to be dirty dancing with any German tourists or sneaking away from us when our back is turned. It seems like a good idea to me."

"Fine. You win. But if anything goes wrong…"

"Yeah, I know, it's my fault," I said, shutting down the laptop. "Come on; let's give them the news."

We walked back into the living room. "You can stay," Liam said to Gavin. "But I've got my eye on you, bud."

Gavin started to protest, but Liam held up his hand. "Let me fill you in." He explained about the death threats, and Gavin's ruddy complexion paled. "That's why he's got two bodyguards here. That's why I tackled you outside and looked through all your stuff. You still want to stay? If you don't, I'll drive you back to Houmt Souk."

"No way," Gavin said. "If my man Karif here is in trouble, I'm staying."

Karif rested his head on Gavin's greasy dreadlocks, and I shivered. Then Karif jumped to his feet. "Come," he said. "I show you my bedroom."

"You can leave your stuff down here," I said, walking over to the dining-room table. "We'll have the maid wash it all tomorrow."

"Cor," Gavin said.

"But you might need these." I tossed the string of yellow condoms to him.

"Thanks, mate," Gavin said, catching them. Then he took Karif's hand, and the two of them scampered upstairs.

"Wine still outside?" Liam asked.

"Yup."

"Good. I could use another couple of glasses."

12 – TRANSFORMATION

The noise in Karif's bedroom went on for a couple of hours. Laughing, yelps, the sound of the bed banging against the wall. There was a break when Karif crooned what sounded like a love song in Arabic, but after the song was over, the fooling around resumed.

"What are they doing in there?" Liam complained, sitting up in bed next to me, his reading glasses on, the laptop computer open in front of him.

"Would you like me to demonstrate?" I asked.

He looked over the tops of his glasses at me. "You know what I mean. Even though there's nothing suspicious about him in this report, I don't trust this guy. Maybe we should alternate shifts downstairs, make sure he doesn't walk off with Karif's wallet and all the electronics in the house."

"We back to preventing the client from making foolish choices?"

"Absolutely. But I agree with you that Gavin looks harmless."

"Dirty but harmless," I said.

A strangled moan came from Karif's bedroom. "Well, either Karif just got his rocks off, or Gavin killed him," Liam said. "Maybe they'll shut up for a while now."

"Doesn't that make you the least bit horny? Hearing them across the hall?"

I reached over to stroke Liam's dick through the soft cotton of the sheet. He looked over his glasses at me again, then pulled them off and set them on the table next to the bed. He closed the laptop and turned to me. "I suppose we could make some noise of our own," he said. "You're a screamer anyway."

"Not a screamer," I protested. "I moan. Whimper, maybe. Not scream."

"Then I'll have to see if I can make you scream." He scrambled over me, flipping me on my stomach across him in the standard spanking posture. Then he slapped my naked butt hard.

"Who's a bad boy?" he said.

My dick pronged up under me, pressing against his thigh.

"Who let the client slip away?"

I buried my head in the pillow as he spanked me again with his open hand.

"Who thought we ought to have sex with the client?" Another slap. My butt began to sting. "Who's been very bad?" he asked, spanking me again. "Let me hear it."

"Me," I said. "I've been bad."

He spanked me again. "Ow!" I yelped.

"Come on; they want to hear it across the hall."

His hand came down on my butt again, and I yelled, "Ow!"

I was ready for another whack when I felt a squirt of something cold right in my ass crack. I knew what that was.

Liam worked the lube into my ass with his index finger. "Yeah," he said. "A bad boy needs to be punished with a very big dick."

I was tempted to point out that, as we'd measured, my dick was bigger than his, but that was not the right thing to say. "Yes, sir," I said.

"Mmm." He grabbed my dick and ground his dick against it as the index finger of his other hand probed my ass. I squirmed and wriggled on his lap, wanting him in me so bad.

I felt a second finger join the first. "Liam, you're torturing me," I panted.

"Say it," he said. "Loud."

"Fuck me."

"Louder! Let those idiots hear it and know that I take care of you."

"Fuck me, Liam!" I shouted. "Please, fuck me!"

"Anything for you, sweetheart," he said, and even though I couldn't see his face, I could feel the grin on it. He slid out from under me, pulled me so that my legs hung off the bed, and positioned himself behind me.

He didn't have to tell me to cry out as he slammed into me. I did that all on my own. "Oh my God, Liam," I yelled. "Oh God!"

Pain radiated like starbursts through my body as he slammed back and forth into me, his pubic hair scratching against my tender ass cheeks, red from the spanking. But quickly that pain turned into sheer pleasure, and I moaned for all I was worth. "Oh, man, you fuck so good," I said, playing to our imagined audience. "Oh yeah, I love the way your dick fills me up."

The friction of my stiff dick against the sheets spurred me to climax, and I howled like a werewolf at a full moon. The orgasm clenched my ass cheeks around Liam's dick, and that pressure brought him off, squirting his hot come up my ass. Since we were both disease-free and monogamous, we'd quickly abandoned condoms for barebacking. We loved that sensation of skin against skin too much to ever go back.

Liam collapsed on top of me, nestling his chest against my back and kissing the nape of my neck. "Think we taught those whippersnappers a thing or two about fucking?" he asked.

"I think they're going to need more lessons." I loved lying there like that, feeling all his weight on me, the way my chest compressed so that it was difficult to breathe. All too soon, though, he flipped off me, turning us so that he was nestled against my back, his limp dick pressed against my tender ass, his arm draped over my chest. There was no more noise from the master bedroom, and we dozed off.

The next morning, Karif came downstairs alone. "Where's Gavin?" I asked. His clothes were still piled next to the washer, so I knew he hadn't left.

"Cleaning up," Karif said. "I bring him breakfast."

"He can come downstairs," I said. "There's no room service at this hotel."

Gavin didn't appear until Liam, Karif, and I were almost finished with breakfast. The transformation was so surprising I almost didn't recognize him. He'd showered away all the grime and shampooed and rinsed and then blow-dried his hair until it hung in shiny waves to his shoulders. The bikini briefs he was wearing must have belonged to Karif, because they were way too small for a guy with his waist and endowment.

"Well, well, if it isn't Mr. Britain 2009," Liam said. "You clean up nicely."

Shed of all the dirt, Gavin looked Karif's age, if not younger. He smiled bashfully. "Lovely shower," he said. "Haven't had one of those in ages." Karif beamed and held out his hand. Gavin took it, kissed it, then sat down next to him and cuddled.

Fortunately Hakim had stocked the refrigerator well, because I ended up frying four eggs and a half dozen rashers of bacon for Gavin, who washed it down with about a liter of orange juice. "Take it easy, big boy," Liam said. "We eat three meals a day around here."

"Haven't had a proper fry-up since I left home," he said.

"When was that?" Liam asked.

"Cor, lemme think. Must be what, six, seven months now."

"What have you been doing all that time?"

"Just hanging about," he said. "Got some work in the fields in France, then shacked up with a bloke in Cannes for a while. Worked my way down to Italy, then jumped a boat over to Tunis. Heard Djerba was pretty, so I hitched a ride along the coast and over the causeway. Been here a couple of days."

After breakfast we all relaxed around the pool for a while. Karif had given up pressing us to go out; he was happy to lounge naked next to Gavin. After a while Liam jumped in the pool and began swimming laps, and a short time later Gavin joined him.

They were both relaxing against the wall of the deep end when Gavin reached out and wrapped his hand around Liam's dick. Liam took hold of Gavin's wrist, and the boy's mouth dropped open, and his fingers released. "This resort is couples only," Liam said conversationally. "You and Karif, me and Aidan. Get it?"

"Yes, sir," Gavin said, reeling back.

"Hey, I'm the only one who gets to say that to Liam," I said. He looked at me, then finally laughed.

I stood up and stretched. "I'm not sure if Alisa is coming today, so I'm going to do you a big favor, Gavin, and wash your clothes for you."

"Thanks, mate."

"Big favor not to me," Karif said. "Now he will have clean clothes. I like him stay naked all the time."

Gavin splashed him, and Karif jumped in to play with him. Liam followed me to the laundry room. "I'm worried about the new threat Yaroush told me about last night," he said, as I gingerly picked up the filthy clothes and dropped them into the washer. "Whoever it is knows we're in Djerba."

"What's up with the threats, anyway?" I asked. "If they know where we are, why not just try something?"

Liam shrugged, then leaned back against the wall. He had a towel wrapped around his waist, his semihard dick pressing against the terry cloth. I wondered if I could lure him up to our bedroom for more fun while the boys were playing in the pool.

"Threats are psychological," he said. "People who send them want their victims to freak out. That's often all the reward they need."

I paused, holding the detergent. "So we shouldn't worry?"

"Nope. I'm worried. And we should be careful, within limits. We've already seen how Karif reacts when he feels like he's a prisoner. A good sniper with an assault rifle could pick him off while he's out by the pool. But if we keep him inside, he'll go nuts."

"Not now that Gavin is here." I poured a cupful of detergent in the washer, closed the lid, and turned it on.

"I still don't trust Gavin. But at least Karif is happy."

I leaned up and kissed him. We'd never made love in a laundry room before; hell, we'd never had access to one before. Back in Tunis, I took our clothes a few blocks away to a laundry, where everything was washed, dried, and ironed for a few dinars a week.

Pulling Liam close to me, I rested my ass against the washer, absorbing its heat and motion into my body. He turned his back to me, dropped his towel, and leaned backward. I wrapped my arms around his waist and pressed my dick against his ass. I kissed his shoulder blades, tasting the pool chlorine and the Tunisian sun on his skin.

My dick stiffened, and precome began to ooze from the tip. With my right hand I reached down for his dick, which was hard too. I wrapped my hand around it, feeling the hood slip back. His dick pulsed with a rhythm like a heartbeat, and I felt so connected to him.

He pressed back against me, stepping up on his toes so that my dick could find its way to his ass. He sighed with contentment as it hit the mark. I began fisting his dick with my right hand, tweaking his nipple with my left.

I kept kissing his neck and shoulders as he bucked his ass against my dick. The washer vibrated against my ass, and I felt almost delirious from so many different sensory inputs at once. I was sure this was going to be an amazing fuck.

Then the house phone rang.

"I'll get it," Liam said, pulling away from me and leaning down for his towel. "We'll pick this up later."

It took me a minute to catch my breath, and even longer for my dick to relax. When it did, I followed Liam to the living room. He looked up from the phone and said, "Yaroush wants to speak to Karif."

I went out to the pool deck, carrying the cordless phone from the kitchen, and handed it to Karif, who was back on his lounge chair. "It's Yaroush."

They spoke in Arabic, so I only caught every third or fourth word. But it was clear that Yaroush wanted something, and Karif didn't want to give it to him. By the end of the call, though, Yaroush had won. I could see it in the slump of Karif's shoulders. He handed the phone back to Liam, and I followed Liam inside.

He spoke with Yaroush in English so that I could understand everything. "I think that's a bad idea, Yaroush," he said, sitting on the sofa. "You're just playing into their hands." He listened for a while. "We weren't anywhere near there," he said. "Or there."

More listening. "Oh. Yeah, we were in Houmt Souk. Someone saw that?" His body language changed. "Okay. Where did you want to do this?"

I looked through the sliding-glass doors at Karif and Gavin.

Karif sat back on his lounge chair, his arms folded in a textbook example of defensive posture. Gavin stood in the pool next to the chair; it looked like he was trying to get Karif to tell him what was going on.

I knew. Someone had seen Karif in Houmt Souk while he'd slipped away from me. Maybe even saw him blowing Gavin in that alley. Did Yaroush know that Gavin was staying at the villa now? Did he want Gavin to leave, and was that what Karif was angry about?

Liam motioned to me for a pen and paper, and I gave them to him. I saw him write down the name of a hotel, and I turned to the laptop and brought up its Web site while he finished the call.

When he hung up, his face was grim. "There's a gossip columnist out of Cairo named Joseph Saad. He's been collecting sightings of Karif and publishing them in his column."

"Let me guess. Somebody saw Karif on his knees in Houmt Souk."

"Yup. Fortunately there were a dozen other sightings on Djerba, so that one is getting lost in the list. Supposedly he gave an impromptu concert on the beach in Aghir. Someone else saw him kissing a man on the ferry from Adjim back to the mainland. He's been seen in the souk at Guellala, the fortress of Borj el-Kebir, and at least five different hotels in the Zone Touristique."

"He gets around. What did Yaroush want that Karif didn't want to give him?"

"The record company is going to fly Joseph Saad to Djerba for an exclusive interview. Karif didn't want to talk, but Yaroush said he had no choice. Talking to the columnist might turn things around, control the publicity."

"So it wasn't about Gavin?"

"I didn't tell Yaroush about Gavin, and I don't think Karif did either. We're keeping our little songbird on the down low for now."

"For as long as we can keep him from giving random blowjobs in public, that is," I said. "When is this interview supposed to take place?"

"Tomorrow. The guy's going to fly in, then spend the weekend at this hotel in Houmt Souk, courtesy of the record company. They hope that will make him want to write nice things about Karif."

"Think it'll work?"

"Not my decision to make. You and I just have to make sure Karif stays safe whatever happens."

13 — QUAD BIKES

Liam and I huddled over the laptop, reading Joseph Saad's online column. Most of the sightings were false, as we knew, and I wondered how many of them Saad himself had manufactured. Though he didn't get down and dirty about the blowjob in the alley in Houmt Souk, he hinted that Karif had been seen in a compromising position with another man.

"Do you think he has someone watching us?" I asked.

"If he did, he'd have much more specific information. He'd have pictures; he'd have gone after Gavin. More likely some fan saw them in the alley and reported it to him, hoping for a reward."

"It's still creepy," I said. "Suppose he's got the villa staked out, and he knows Gavin is here. Imagine what those pictures would do to Karif's career."

"I think we're still safe here. We've got a clear view from the back of the property. We'd be able to spot anybody, even with a long-range lens. Though it means we have to be extra careful when we're out."

Alisa came in then, and I told her about the laundry, and Liam took bathing suits to the young lovers. While Alisa cleaned the kitchen and living room, we all sat by the pool, and when she went upstairs, we came back inside.

The boys cuddled on the sofa, and Liam went back to the computer, trying to find out as much as possible about the hotel where the interview would take place. I knew that he would go over there himself, speak to the manager, and evaluate all the potential risks. Then we'd play the "what-if" game for a while together. What if someone tried to attack Karif at the hotel? What if Joseph Saad himself tried something? What if we had to leave the hotel fast -- how would we get out? Where would we leave the Land Rover; what road would we take?

The planning was the most important part of the job. The more we knew in advance, the easier it would be to prevent trouble or to react if anything happened.

While I waited for Liam to finish, I turned on the TV; it was a luxury for me, because we had no TV at our house. With the satellite dish on the roof, we were able to pull in stations from all over the Arab world, and I wanted to practice understanding spoken Arabic.

I flipped through channels, past a travelogue, a music video, and a horse race in Dubai. When I found a news station, I began to pay attention. The third or fourth story was a report of a demonstration in Beirut. I was trying to figure out what the story was about, the boys giggling and teasing each other, when Liam looked up from his computer.

"Turn that up," he said. "You guys, quiet."

We all turned to the TV. From what I could tell, a man had been killed, and an Islamic militant group had claimed credit. As we watched, they broadcast photos of several other men.

"That's you, mate," Gavin said, elbowing Karif when his picture appeared.

"Quiet," Liam ordered. Karif's mouth dropped open, and his eyes widened.

"Now you see why you need protection?" Liam said to him when the spot was finished. He took the remote and flipped the TV off.

"What's going on?" Gavin asked.

"A gay activist was shot and killed in Beirut," Liam said. "They were showing Karif's picture because they were pointing out all the gay men who've had threats against them."

Karif began to shiver and cry, and Gavin wrapped a beefy arm around him. "They'll have to get through me to get to you, mate." He looked at us. "They're not really serious, are they?"

"Why do you think Karif has two armed bodyguards?" I asked him. "Wake up, Gavin."

"Armed?" he said. "You mean like guns?"

"Yes, Gavin." Liam was lost in thought, so it was up to me to carry the conversation. I softened my tone. "We did go through this last night. Now you see, we weren't kidding."

Karif pulled away from Gavin's arm, huddling against the arm of the sofa. "You go please, Gavin," he said. "I am not want you hurt."

From Gavin's openmouthed stare, I could see he was having trouble processing it all. "We'll drive you back to Houmt Souk," I said gently. "Karif's right. None of us want you to get hurt."

Gavin sat up straight on the sofa. "I grew up in Sheffield," he said. "Tough town for a boy who likes other boys. I was all right, you know, 'cause I played sports and fooled around with girls. This other lad, Nigel, wasn't so lucky. The yobs used to pick on him something fierce 'cause they could see he was a nelly boy. Once they caught him wearing his ma's makeup and broke his nose."

Liam looked up from his computer, and all three of us were watching Gavin. "I felt right lousy that I didn't stick up for him, but I didn't want those yobs coming after me." He reached out his arm for Karif and pulled him close. "Not going to do that again. I'm tough. Don't know anything about guns, but I've got fists. Whatever you need me for, I'm here."

My eyes stung as Karif nestled into Gavin's chest, Gavin's wavy hair falling over Karif's head and shoulders.

Alisa came downstairs then and went to the laundry room. "Come into the kitchen," Liam said to me. I followed him there, and he said, "We've got to do something to keep them occupied today. I don't want Karif sitting around stewing over that report or worrying about the interview."

"Can't we just lock them up in Karif's bedroom and let them fuck their brains out?"

"Read the body language," Liam said, positioning me in the doorway to look back at the boys. "Tell me what you see."

"Gavin has his arm around Karif. They're cuddling."

"Is it sexual?"

"How am I supposed to know?"

"You've got to look," Liam said. "See the way Karif still has his arms wrapped around himself? He's scared. And the way Gavin's not looking at him? He's confused. We lock them upstairs, they're just going to brood at each other."

I saw what Liam was seeing. "How did you get so perceptive about people?"

"Lots of time paying attention. Go online and see if you can find something active we can do. They're like Hayam -- keep them busy and you'll keep them out of trouble."

I wanted to smile at the reference to our dog, the way we walked her all around Tunis so she'd be too tired to tear anything up. But Liam was serious, and I had to be too.

"I'm going to run over to the hotel and check out the security," Liam said.

While he was gone, I went online, looking up options, and soon I had an idea. Alisa left and the boys went back out to the pool, and I could see what Liam had meant -- each was lost in his own thoughts. When I finished my research, I tried to rope them into helping me fix lunch, but without success.

By the time Liam returned, I had put together a salad with chopped chicken and some fresh-baked rolls from a mix. I pulled him aside as the boys were picking at their food, neither of them demonstrating much appetite.

"What would you think about quad bikes?" I asked. "Karif saw an ad for them at the airport, and he sounded interested back then."

"I think it would work," Liam said, looking at the information I'd printed out. "We'll be out in the country, away from people." There was a rental place in Midoun that took you out for an hour-and-a-half tour, and after confirming they were open and had availability, Liam made a reservation for us.

"You guys want to go out on quad bikes?" Liam asked, coming back into the kitchen.

Karif raised his head. "I am seeing that at the airport! But what it is?"

"Like a motorcycle, but for the countryside." Liam pretended to rev a bike at the handlebars and said, "Vroom, vroom."

The boys laughed. "All right, then. Let's get moving," Liam said. We all scrambled to get dressed, skipping showers because we'd just get dirty and sweaty on the bikes. I wrangled the boys into the Land Rover as Liam threw a duffle in the back.

I wondered if he'd brought our guns, binoculars, or some other equipment he didn't want to talk about in front of the boys. On the ride to Midoun, he told a story about quad biking himself. "I can't tell you the country we started in or the one we crossed into," he said. "But I'll tell you that our heads were wrapped in scarves and we were camouflaged as Bedouins. We mounted these ATVs that were at least twenty years old, leaking oil and smoking like chimneys and followed camel trails in the middle of the night. We had some explosives to plant, and the whole time I was worried I'd take a header on some dune and the C4 would go off."

"You were being bodyguard then?" Karif asked.

Liam shook his head. "Back when I was a US Navy SEAL. Long time ago."

"Cor, you were one of those?" Gavin asked. "I seen them on TV."

"Don't believe everything you see on the little box," Liam said as he pulled up in front of a storefront with a slew of bikes on racks out front. I checked us in with a skinny Tunisian guy in a Metallica concert T-shirt. Then he explained how to drive the bikes and fitted us for helmets.

When he had us all on bikes, our guide raised his hand, revved his bike, and took off. Karif went right after the guide, then Gavin, then me, with Liam at the rear. I had trouble getting my balance on the sandy road, and I nearly wiped out but managed to save myself by holding the bike steady, squeezing the handlebars till my fingers felt frozen in place. Some bodyguard, I thought.

Liam, of course, could do almost anything, and he rode the quad bike like he had been born to it. For a while we followed a sandy track through a desert area with high banks on either side. We passed a couple of traditional white stucco houses with domed roofs, and a lot of cacti. We couldn't drive very fast here, as we had to negotiate the turns, but suddenly we were out on the wide-open beach with compact sand, and our guide revved his engine and took off.

The boys were right behind him, though I lagged until I got accustomed to going faster. Liam passed me, waving his hand, so that he could stay on their tail. I felt abandoned, watching him speed ahead, and didn't notice the big rock looming ahead of me until it was almost too late.

I panicked and only managed to turn the wheel just in time. I throttled down and pulled aside, panting, my heart racing. I couldn't see the guide, the boys, or Liam ahead of me. Sweat dripped down my forehead, and the helmet was so close that I felt a headache coming on.

How stupid was I, to think I could manage a job like Liam's? I'd been through that bodyguard training in Atlanta, but our teachers had told us, over and over again, to expect simple jobs at first. Standing guard in a hallway or near an elevator. *"You won't get near the client for a year or more,"* one teacher had said. *"Get used to that. If you're in this for the glamour, you're in the wrong place."*

I had done a few small jobs with Liam, researching locations, driving clients, and so on. I wished I'd had more practice like that before I had been thrust in the middle of something as complex as keeping Karif Al-Fulan safe from death threats.

Yet here I was, on assignment, with unknown assassins waiting for the chance to kill our client. In the far distance I saw a hotel beach, a couple of umbrellas, and lounge chairs, the sun glinting on some random piece of metal.

Was I going to be a wimp, wait for someone to come back and find me? Or was I going to man up, start the bike once more, and chase after them? There wasn't much choice, was there? I revved the bike, set my feet on the pedals, and leaned forward.

I went slow for a few hundred yards, then gradually added speed until I was flying. I could see why people liked this; once I got comfortable, I reveled in the feeling of the wind and the ocean spray as I soared over the sand. I was hoping the boys were enjoying it as much as I was.

If only Liam and I had been sharing a bike! I wanted to cuddle up behind him, wrap my legs around him, and press my groin to his butt, feeling the power of the motorcycle beneath me. I kept having to remind myself that we weren't on vacation, that this was a job -- with deadly consequences if we failed. Even so, it sure beat teaching English as a Second Language back in Philadelphia.

I caught up with the rest of the group at an overlook where the beach curved. "What happened to you?" Liam asked, pulling me aside. "I can't worry about you and the client too."

Something in his tone rankled me. "I know I'm not as strong or as capable as you, but you don't have to treat me like a child," I said. "I had a little trouble with the bike, but I got over it."

"I need to know I can depend on you. Otherwise you're just in the way."

My voice rose. "Excuse me? I'm in your way?"

The boys looked over at us, and Liam glared at me. Then his shoulders relaxed. "I'm sorry," he said. "I was worried about you. And I can't be worrying about what's up with you when I'm trying to take care of the client."

"Welcome to my world. I worry about you all the time. I know how capable you are and I trust you and all that -- but I still worry every time you go out on a case and I'm not there with you."

"Come take pictures," Karif called.

Liam smiled and put his arm around me. "Duty calls," he said. None of us had a camera beyond the built-in one in our phones. We snapped a couple of shots, Liam careful that there could be nothing incriminating in the poses between Karif and Gavin.

Then the guide motioned us back to the bikes, and we turned inland, where we stopped at a café for cups of mint tea. The four of us settled down at a table in the shade of a pair of date palms, while our guide stayed back in the café to gossip with the owner.

A little girl approached us, a flyer of some sort in her hand. I assumed she was looking for a handout and nodded to Liam. But she went right to Karif and asked, in Arabic, if she could have his autograph.

So much for anonymity, I thought. Karif borrowed a pen from the café owner and signed the paper for the girl -- and then everyone around us caught on, and he had five or six more requests for autographs.

No one said anything about his recent outing, but the cluster of fans around him made me nervous. They were so close to him; any one of them could have slid a knife between his ribs before Liam or I could react. Liam was on full alert, and it looked like he wanted to pull Karif away. But too strong a show of force could destroy the moment, make Karif feel more in danger, and provide fodder for ugly news stories.

Gavin watched the whole episode with a bemused smile. Even though he'd seen Karif's face on TV, listened to his CD, heard us describe the death threats, I think he hadn't fully believed Karif was a celebrity.

Karif's last autograph was for a gruff, older Arab man who said his daughter played Karif's CD all the time. Karif smiled and wrote a personal note to her, then handed it back to the man.

"Now, you go find yourself a nice girl!" the man admonished in Arabic that was basic enough for me to understand. "No more fooling around!"

I worried how Karif would react -- but all he did was give the man a mock, two-fingered salute from his forehead, saying, "Will do, sir!"

14 – STEAMY SITUATION

"Who wants to go to a hammam?" Liam asked as we walked away from returning the quad bikes. I thought that was a perfect idea; my back and shoulders ached from leaning over the bike handlebars, and dirt and sand had lodged in every pore. "There's a nice one at a hotel in Houmt Souk, with sauna, pools, even massages."

"Yes, please," Karif asked. "I am very dirty." He looked at Gavin. "For you, this is normal, no?"

Gavin elbowed him. "I'll show you dirty, mate."

"We'd need clean clothes," I said.

"Already got them," Liam said. "In the duffle."

Oh. No weapons or sophisticated defensive stuff. Just clean clothes. "Where's this hammam?" I asked.

"The Hotel Grand Djerba. It's on the edge of town, on the water. It's where Joseph Saad is staying. Thought it would be a good idea to do some recon."

It was already late afternoon by then. As Liam drove, I called ahead to the hotel and made the arrangements. The hammam was segregated by sex; Liam had already checked to be sure it was a men's day.

The Hotel Grand Djerba was a two-story sprawl of glittering white stucco, with domed roofs and elaborate tiled archways. Liam pulled up to the front door and handed the car over to the valet. "I'm going to check things out," he said to me. "I'll be there soon."

The doorman directed us down a covered breezeway lined with twisted columns to the hammam entrance. I'd only been in one of these Turkish baths before, in a small town out in the desert, and this one was much fancier. A young man in a beige uniform with red epaulets led us to the locker room, issuing us towels and keys to tall metal lockers.

We wrapped the towels around our waists, and I said, "No sex play," to Karif and Gavin. "Remember, this is a public place. We don't need to start any more Internet rumors."

Our attendant waited while we stripped, then led us to a tiled shower room, as nice as any luxury hotel bathroom. Waist-high walls separated each showerhead, and shelves built into the wall offered a range of products, from body wash to shampoo and conditioner.

As I began to shower, Liam slipped into the stall across from me. "I did some quick recon," he said, as he turned the water on. "Tell you about it later."

The first time I saw Liam, I was in the Bar Mamounia in Tunis, looking through an opening in the wall that passed for a window. Liam was showering beneath a hose rigged from a cistern on his roof, in a small courtyard that separated the bar from his house.

Water streamed from his muscular, sun-browned body. He'd looked like a Greek god come to life, the sun glinting on his nipple rings, and it was lust at first sight for me. My dick stiffened, and I felt powerless with longing. I didn't approach him then, but I couldn't get that picture out of my mind, and I went back to the bar the next day.

He mistook me for a client he was supposed to meet, and that coincidence threw us together and sent us spiraling off through the desert. By the time we returned from that adventure, we were in love, and I moved in with him.

In the shower at the hotel hammam, I could tell Liam knew I was looking at him. His long, fat dick bobbed against his thigh, semihard, as he lathered up his pecs, raising his arms to scrub his pits. He smiled at me, tracing lazy circles with a handful of shower gel across his flat stomach.

My dick stood up at attention as I followed his lead, scrubbing away the dirt and grime of the quad-bike ride. He turned his back to me, leaning his face up to the showerhead, the water streaming down over his shoulder blades. I longed to cross the few feet that separated us, soap up his back, press my stiff dick against his succulent ass.

But I had to be satisfied with watching him pry open his ass, lather his hole with the foamy gel, then rinse it out. I bent down to scrub a dirty streak on my right shin, and when I looked up again, I saw Liam focused across the way, at where Gavin was showering next to me.

Because of the wall between us, I couldn't see anything more of Gavin than his head and shoulders, but it looked like there was something lower that Liam found awful fascinating.

Karif and Gavin finished first, and they wrapped themselves in their towels and stepped out of the shower. As Liam and I walked out behind them, I said in a low voice, "You said we couldn't have sex with Karif because we'd be prostituting ourselves. But does that rule apply to Gavin?"

Liam pulled me aside. "You actually want to have sex with that idiot?"

"Don't you think he's cute? You know I like my men with meat on them."

"Really? Because I saw your ex-boyfriend when he showed up at my door chasing after you. He was damned skinny."

"How about you?" I asked as we started walking again. "You think Gavin is cute?"

"I think you're just trying to irritate me," Liam said. "Hurry up. I don't like having those two out of my sight for long. You don't know what kind of trouble they'll get into."

So whatever Liam had been looking at in the shower, it didn't seem like he was lusting after Gavin. I felt great as we stepped out of the shower and the attendant led the four of us to a small, wood-paneled sauna. He set the timer outside for fifteen minutes and pantomimed that he would return when we were finished.

The heat was heavy and moist, like being slapped in the face with a steamy towel. We sat on slatted benches, leaning forward, as the steam cleansed our pores. I felt all the tension of the bike ride, the whole assignment, slipping away. Gavin began to cough after a few minutes. "Hard to breathe in here," he said.

"Take shallow breaths," Liam said. "Breathe through your mouth. You'll get accustomed to it." For a minute or two I thought we'd all have to leave, but Gavin managed to control his breathing. I watched him carefully, though, just to be sure, but after a while I had to look away because the sight of those droplets of sweat slipping off his beefy pecs was getting me hard again.

What a slut I was, I thought. I already had the most handsome man in the world -- Liam. He was an enthusiastic sex partner; he gave up every inch of his body to me, tried anything I wanted. He knew how to use his muscles to control his own reactions and mine.

One day we had experimented, trying to see how long we could make love without either of us coming to orgasm. He sucked me, then pulled off. Then I sucked him until I felt his dick begin to boil with gathering semen. We went back and forth like that for nearly two hours, each of us determined to hold out longer than the other. I began to beg him to finish me, writhing with desire, and when he wouldn't oblige, I tormented him too. By the time we both gave in, my body was rocked by an orgasm so complete, so painful and yet so amazing, that I nearly passed out.

So why was I turned on by Gavin and Karif? Was I simply a slave to my hormones? Was I ever going to grow up? I wasn't a horny kid like Gavin or fresh out of the closet like Karif. I was over thirty, a responsible adult.

I remembered Francisco Bell, an older man I knew in Philadelphia whose Spanish nickname was Paco. He was another ESL teacher I often had coffee with during a break between classes. Paco was nearly sixty and loved to leer at every handsome guy who passed by. At first I thought he was just plain sad. But as I got to know him better, I learned he had a longtime partner and what sounded like a pretty satisfying sex life with him.

"It never hurts to look," he'd said to me. "Keeps me young. And that way I know the equipment, including the brain, is still working."

With luck, I figured I'd end up like Paco Bell -- happy at home and still enjoying the view.

When the timer went off, the four of us left the sauna for a large, domed room with a skylight that flooded sunshine over the pool at the center. A series of benches ran around the perimeter of the room on a raised platform. Liam dropped his soggy towel at the water's edge and led the way into the pool, jumping in feetfirst, then bobbing back up to the surface, the water cascading off his head and shoulders.

The rest of us followed. There were two other men already in the pool area, older Europeans relaxing on the benches, and they looked on as we splashed and romped in the pool. The attendant was waiting with fresh towels as we climbed out.

"Who's ready for a massage?" Liam asked after speaking to the attendant. "We should go two at a time."

"Gavin and I will go," Karif said.

Liam shook his head. "I'll go with you, and Aidan can go with Gavin. Remember, we're in charge of your safety."

Karif pouted but let himself be led away with Liam as Gavin and I climbed to take seats on the bench. "This is fucking amazing," Gavin said, leaning back against the wall. "Two nights ago I was sleeping rough on the beach in Houmt Souk. And now I'm here."

"What's your story, Gavin?" I asked. "You just picked up one day and went walkabout?"

He shrugged. "Had some trouble back home. Decided it was

time for a change of scenery."

"What kind of trouble?"

"You know."

"No, Gavin, I don't know. But I can find out if I want." We had done a basic search on Gavin when he showed up at the villa, which raised no red flags. But there were more elaborate, expensive searches we could do if we thought something was fishy, including convincing someone to release information on Gavin's criminal record, if he had one.

He looked away, then finally back. "I don't want Karif to know. Don't want him to think bad of me."

"Let's talk about what you don't want him to know. And then figure out how to tell him. Because keeping secrets never leads to a happy ending."

He wiped some sweat from his forehead. "I never was much good in school. Squeaked out of grammar school with a couple of A levels, nothing good enough to go to uni."

"Uh-huh."

"I did a couple of dodgy things. Sold some dope, shoplifted, got picked up by the old bill a few times."

"That why you left? Running from the cops?"

He shook his head. "Not really."

"Gavin. Spit it out."

"I was on the game, all right?" he said. "Toffs wanting a bit of rough, but not too rough. I worked for this bloke, see, and he had a couple of us lads. Johnny was black. Nigel was twenty, at least, but looked fifteen. Steven had a posh accent. Each of us different, you know?"

"I can see how you might be ashamed. But I think Karif would understand."

"It weren't just the sex," Gavin said, his voice low. "They give us drugs and sometimes made us work together, do downright nasty things."

Gavin's bravado had been stripped away, and I saw fear and sadness beneath the cheerful front he presented. It looked like he was about to say something else when Liam and Karif returned. "Your turn," Liam said.

The attendant led us to another room down the hall, this one at least ten degrees cooler than the pool area. Two Arab men wearing the hotel uniform stood by long marble-topped tables. I drew the skinnier of the two, who commanded me to lie face down on his table.

I stretched out against the marble slab, ready for a relaxing massage, when the man began to rub a glove that felt like steel wool against my back. I yelped, hearing Gavin react the same way, but the man pushed my shoulders back toward the bench and kept on rubbing.

It was a coarse loofah, I figured out as he made me sit up, then lie on my back, and I saw flakes of dead skin rolling off. I began to enjoy the process, my skin taking on a rosy glow. When he finished, the masseur rubbed olive oil soap over my body. I smelled like a tossed salad.

He poured buckets of cool water over me until I was completely clean. He used the sides of his arms to press deep into my muscles; then all his weight came down on my back, flattening me against the stone until I felt thin as a sheet of phyllo pastry. My arms and legs were bent into a dozen different directions, and it sounded like every vertebra in my spine cracked.

When he slapped me on the back, I sat up and flexed. My body felt loose and limber as Gavin and I walked back to the pool room. We took one more dip in the pool, wrapped ourselves in fresh towels, then joined Karif and Liam against the wall.

The attendant brought us all cups of mint tea. As I sipped mine, I looked at Gavin and considered what he'd told me. I knew there was something else there. Was he running from a vengeful pimp? From the police? Was he still using drugs? I'd have to pass on what I'd learned to Liam, and I'd have to do that advanced search I had threatened Gavin with.

There was a chance, given whatever it was in his background he was worried about confessing, that someone had gotten to him, sent him to us to make an attempt on Karif's life. Yet he'd had plenty of opportunity and had done nothing.

His best chance had been when he had Karif alone in the alley in Houmt Souk; he could have put a knife in his ribs or knocked him out with a paving block. Once ensconced in the villa with us, he could have slipped poison into Karif's wine, or smothered Karif as he slept, then slid away under the cover of darkness.

He hadn't done any of those, but that didn't mean he wasn't

biding his time, waiting for the right opportunity. I looked across to where he sat with Karif, joking and teasing. Or he could just be a cute, horny guy exercising his hormones. It was going to be up to Liam and me to figure out which was true.

15 – DRAWING A CROWD

We ate dinner there at the Hotel Grand Djerba, getting back to the villa well after dark. The boys were happy and tired by then, all those terrible thoughts spurred by the morning newscast swept away. They went up to Karif's room, and over glasses of wine I told Liam about Gavin's background as I opened up the laptop.

Liam had worked with a bodyguard from a big firm in France on a couple of cases, and that guy had passed us some very interesting software as well as codes that got us into most law enforcement databases. We didn't like to use them frequently, though, because we didn't want to take unnecessary risks.

As Liam sipped his wine, I did some searching on Gavin Jones. With the information from his passport, I was able to turn up criminal records that jived with what he'd told me.

"But you think there's something he's not saying," Liam said, looking over my shoulder.

"Just a hunch." We were both worn-out from the overall stress of the assignment, our quad-biking adventure, and then the massage, so we went up to bed, cuddled together for a few minutes, then went to sleep.

When I woke the next morning around seven, Liam was already awake and getting dressed. "What's up?" I asked, yawning.

"I didn't get to do as much recon at the hotel as I wanted yesterday, so I'm going back there, to see what it's like during the day.

Joseph Saad is supposed to check in this morning, and I'd like to get into his room before he does."

"You're going to plant a recorder?"

"I don't think he'll let you or me sit in on the interview, but I want to know what they talk about. I'm going to get into his room and place a voice-activated transmitter so that once they start talking, we can listen in."

We had brought with us a couple of transmitters, small enough to be placed inconspicuously in Saad's room, as well as a receiver, like a handheld walkie-talkie, we could use to monitor the conversation.

"How are you going to retrieve the device once you plant it?" I asked.

"Not sure. We'll have to monitor the situation. Maybe we can draw Saad out of his room after he and Karif have finished talking."

I shook my head. "He's going to be writing up the interview. And we won't want to wait around the hotel until he's done. Have you considered using Karif?"

"We don't have the equipment to wire him up. Plus he'll be nervous enough about the interview."

"We don't have to wire him, do we? Couldn't we just give him the pen to carry?" I'd learned about a nifty little transmitter concealed in a pen when I was in bodyguard school. I'd bought one as a gift for Liam when I stopped over in London on my way home from Atlanta.

"He'd better bring it back," Liam said.

"If he doesn't, we'll put it on his tab."

Liam left a little later, and after breakfast the boys spent most of the morning in the pool. The exercise, the massage, and the night's sleep had done a good job of restoring their high spirits, and they splashed and tickled each other, necking and fondling each other like they were in some low-budget porn flick. Maybe *Dicks Dallying in Djerba*. Or *Poolside Penis Party*.

I had to get my head back in the game and stop imagining porno flicks, so I pulled out my laptop and began researching Joseph Saad. He was one of the best-known gossip columnists in the Arab world, though I didn't recognize most of the names in his columns. But it appeared that he specialized in scandalous stories about movie stars, singers, athletes, and politicians. When an Egyptian actress was spotted with a black eye, Saad had pictures and interviews with her maid, who swore the actress had been fighting with her boyfriend, an unemployed assistant director she'd met on her last movie.

When a minor Saudi prince stiffed a London hotel for a six-figure bill, Saad had interviewed the management. When a Lebanese official was found dead in his Rome hotel room, Saad tracked down the hooker who had tied him up and then skedaddled when he suffered a heart attack.

I hoped, for Saad's sake, that the picture accompanying his column didn't do him justice. He had a round face, tiny eyes, and a chin beard that reminded me of the Billy Goats Gruff.

Around midmorning, when I couldn't read any more scandal, I checked on the boys out by the pool. Karif sat up on his lounge chair, crying. Gavin had his arm around him, and when I came to the sliding-glass doors, Gavin looked up at me and shook his head ever so slightly.

I went back to the computer and switched to a study of the hotel, memorizing its layout, closing my eyes to visualize moving around inside. Every half hour or so I looked out at the pool, where the sun was relentlessly bright, the sky the same cloudless blue it had been since our arrival. Karif had recovered from whatever had bothered him and lay on his lounge chair, tanning as Gavin frolicked in the pool.

Liam was back just before noon, as I was making lunch. "Did you find anything interesting?" I asked.

He leaned back against the counter as I pulled a tray of garlic bread out of the oven. "Saad's in a suite on the second floor, at the end of the hall, which is good. I'll stay outside his door, and you can position yourself in the garden below his window. That way both of us can listen in."

I asked him to lay the fragrant bread out on a tray while I drained the pasta.

"The hotel manager knows we're bringing Karif in, and he'll have someone ready to take us up the back stairs right to Saad's room," he said as he decanted the pasta into a bowl and began tossing it with sun-dried tomatoes, artichoke hearts, and olive oil.

"Sounds like you got a lot accomplished," I said, laying plates out on the table.

"I also talked to the security manager, Ilias Bouchta. He'll have his guys scan everyone who comes into the hotel while we're there. It's not perfect, because an assassin could already be in place -- but it's the best we can do for now."

He carried the pasta to the table and started dishing it out. "How were the boys this morning?"

"Okay, I guess." I told him how I'd seen Karif crying. "Gavin's good for him. He's turning out to be a sweetheart."

"Assuming whatever it is he's hiding doesn't matter," Liam said. "I'm still not sure I trust him. I wouldn't be surprised to see him head right to the tabloids if Karif kicks him to the curb."

I couldn't argue with that; I had my doubts about Gavin too, and money could be a powerful lure, especially when you're nursing a broken heart. Even if Gavin was the one to leave in the end.

"We need to keep Gavin away from Joseph Saad," I said. "And Karif's got to keep his mouth shut. I can just see the headlines -- *Arab singer in beachfront love shack with British rent boy.*"

"You have a colorful imagination." Liam called the boys in while I poured glasses of lemonade for everyone. "We've got to leave here in half an hour," he said as they sat down. "Karif, I need you showered and dressed by then. Gavin, you're going to stay behind."

"No!" Karif said. "I want Gavin come." He reached across the table and took Gavin's hand.

Liam shook his head. "You know that's a bad idea, Karif. Yaroush will have our heads if Saad finds out Gavin is staying here with you and splashes it all over his newspaper."

"I am not saying about Gavin," Karif said. "He wait by pool or in restaurant. But nearby, please."

His voice was shaky, and I could see him squeezing Gavin's

hand. Both of them looked to us.

"You understand the consequences, Karif?" I asked. "If you tell Joseph Saad you have a boyfriend, you'll stir up the controversy again. You'll be stuck here forever, and you'll never get that US tour you want."

"I am understanding," Karif said. "But frightened. Please?"

I looked at Liam.

He sighed. "All right. But we do this my way. I'll be with you, and Aidan will keep Gavin out of sight."

"Yes, that is fine," Karif said. He turned to Gavin. "Is okay with you?"

"You bet, sweetheart." He leaned in to kiss Karif on the cheek.

Karif and Gavin went upstairs to get ready. "I don't want Gavin or Karif to know we're listening to the interview, so you won't be able to have a headset," Liam said. "I'll record everything so we can listen to it again back here."

We went back over the map of the Hotel Grand Djerba's property one last time so that the exits, the parking lot, and the places where Gavin and I could wait while Karif was interviewed and still be within radio contact were familiar to both of us. It was going to be a touchy operation, keeping Karif safe and at the same time keeping Gavin out of sight.

When Karif came downstairs, I said, "You might need a pen and paper while you're talking to Saad." I handed him the transmitter pen and a small pad. "Here, put this in your pocket. But this is Liam's favorite pen, so be sure to bring it back."

He accepted them without argument, holding Gavin's hand as we walked out to the Land Rover.

Liam said, "Aidan, I want you to drive. Gavin, you get in the front seat, and Karif and I will get in the back."

Karif looked ready to complain, but Liam glared at him. I drove slowly down the coast road, stopping frequently to let tourists in bathing suits and flip-flops cross in front of us. We passed an olive grove stretching off into the horizon, sandwiched between a modern white stucco hotel and the ruins of a stone fort with a single turret still intact. Building signs were in Arabic and Roman script -- even the stop sign, in the traditional red octagon, had the English word beneath the Arabic.

No one spoke on the trip to Houmt Souk until we were pulling in the driveway at the Hotel Grand Djerba. We were about a half hour early; Liam hoped that might put Joseph Saad at a disadvantage.

"Drop me and Karif at the front door," Liam said. "Then I want you to leave the hotel, do a big circle around the town, and come back no sooner than ten minutes, all right?"

"Why is that?" Karif demanded.

"In case anyone is watching," Liam said. "I don't want them to see all four of us. That all right with you?"

In the rearview mirror, I saw Karif nod.

"You stay in the car until I come around and open the door for you," Liam said to Karif. "I won't let you out until I'm sure it's safe."

I stole a glance at Gavin next to me. His ruddy face was pale, and he was gripping the door handle. Once again I worried that he might have his own reasons for being with Karif, reasons that had nothing to do with the pop singer's dick or ass.

But everyone behaved. I pulled up at the front entrance and waved the bellman away as he tried to open Gavin's door. Liam got out, walked around the car, and spoke to the bellman, who stepped back. Liam took a good long look around, then opened the door for Karif. "Ten minutes, remember," he said to me.

"Got it. You want me to radio you when we get back?"

"I'll radio you when I have Karif delivered to Joseph Saad," he said. "I'll be outside Saad's door, and then I'll radio you again as we're leaving so you can pick us up out front."

"It's going to be fine," I said to Karif before he stepped out of the car. "Gavin and I will be waiting for you when you're done."

They walked into the hotel, and I drove back down the semicircular drive, then waited for a break in traffic so I could pull out.

"This is right scary," Gavin said as I turned onto the Rue Ulysse toward the Borj el-Kebir, the ancient fort. "You really think Karif's in danger?"

"There's always a chance," I said. "Part of guarding a principal is keeping anybody who might want to harm him guessing where he'll be when. That's why we showed up early today, in case anyone wanted to ambush Karif at the hotel."

"Cor," Gavin said, shaking his head.

I thought about offering him the chance to get out -- but when I looked over at him, he wasn't afraid; he was determined. He was staring straight ahead, his right hand curled into a fist.

I drove slowly through the narrow streets, keeping an eye on my watch. We passed carpet souks with multicolored rugs hanging outside, pottery souks full of vases and couscoussières, and tourist shops selling postcards and T-shirts. The ten minutes had passed as I turned back onto the Rue Ulysse a couple of blocks down from the Hotel Grand Djerba.

"What's going on up there?" Gavin asked, leaning forward.

A crowd was gathering around the entrance to the hotel. "Shit," I said. I risked trying Liam on the radio, but we were out of range.

"You think they're after Karif?" Gavin asked.

"Only one way to tell," I said. Traffic inched forward as cars and hotel vans zigzagged around the growing crowd, mostly men in white shirts and round white caps. A few older women wore traditional blue head scarves. They were waving signs written in shaky Arabic, which I couldn't decipher. But I could hear a few of the words they were shouting: wafat and mamhoon. Death and homosexual. Not a good combination for us.

"What are they saying?"

I didn't want to worry Gavin, so I fibbed. "Can't tell. My Arabic isn't good enough."

"But is it about Karif?"

"That much I can tell."

"How did they bloody know he was here?" Gavin demanded.

"The newspaper reporter must have sabotaged him. Better story that way. Imagine the headlines if Karif gets killed and Joseph Saad is right on the scene. That would be a big boost to his career."

"How do we get him out?"

"I'm thinking." For a moment my brain went blank, as if I'd never gone to bodyguard school, never spent any time listening to Liam talk about tactics. All I could do was keep on driving, inching past the hotel entrance.

The crowd didn't look violent, just angry. But that could change in a second. I noticed a decorative pile of polished white stones at the entrance to the hotel drive. It wouldn't take much for someone in the crowd to pick one up and hurl it at Karif -- or at the Land Rover if he was inside.

"We have to do something," Gavin insisted.

"I know, Gavin. I'm thinking." I had to turn the wheel sharply to avoid a young man in a sleeveless T-shirt who darted in front of me to join the crowd, a long, narrow stick in his hand.

Despite having the air-conditioning on high, I was sweating like mad, gripping the steering wheel. Police were already blocking the driveway into the hotel, so I kept going.

"Oi," Gavin said. "That was the driveway."

"Shut the fuck up, all right?" I turned onto the Rue du Port, heading inland once again, and pulled off into a tiny lot as soon as I could. I fumbled around until I found the map of the hotel grounds and spread it out on my lap. Gavin looked over at it.

This was what I'd been training for, I thought. I couldn't rely on Liam, only on my own instincts. I had to hope they were good enough.

16 — BOAT RIDE

"Let's assume we can't drive up, retrieve them, and drive away," I said to Gavin as I looked down at the map in front of me.

"Why not?"

"First rule of bodyguarding. Keep the client away from the trouble."

I traced my finger down along the hotel's beachfront. There was a kiosk at the water's edge where you could rent Jet Skis and scuba gear. You could also sign up for waterskiing lessons. "That's it," I said, putting my finger on it.

I pulled out my cell phone and called the Hotel Grand Djerba, asking for Ilias Bouchta, the director of security Liam had met with that morning. "I am most sorry," he said once they had brought him to the phone. "I am not having any idea how these people have arrived. It is very distressing."

I told him what I wanted. "Yes," he said. "It can be arranged."

"I'll call you back when we're in place."

I swung back out into traffic, swerving to avoid a pair of backpackers on mopeds, and headed to the port. I pulled into the public parking lot, cruising up and down the aisles until I found the kind of spot I wanted.

"You want to stay here with the car?" I asked Gavin as I shut the Land Rover's engine off.

"No way, mate," he said. "I'm with you."

We hoofed it out to Rue Ulysse, where we hailed a taxi to take us the half mile down to the Hotel Grand Djerba. He wasn't happy with such a short fare, especially not as we got close and he saw the crowds, but I handed him money and promised more once he got us inside.

The baksheesh motivated him, and he nosed the cab through the crowd, blowing his horn and waving his fist, until he reached the police officers at the driveway. The officers looked inside the cab, pegged us as tourists, and waved him through.

"*Shukran,*" I said to the cabbie, handing him more bills. He took the money, grinning, then picked up another fare as we got out.

I knew Liam was supposed to radio me, but I didn't want to wait. As we walked through the lobby, I tried to raise him.

"Where are you?" he asked as Gavin and I sat down at a ceramic-topped table at the edge of the outdoor bar. "I've been trying you. I said ten minutes."

I told him about the crowd outside the hotel. "Where's the car?" he asked.

"I've got an idea." I ran it past him.

"That'll work," he said. "Assuming Bouchta isn't the one who ratted Karif out."

"He didn't have the time. You only spoke to him this morning."

"We'll have to trust him," Liam said. "Hold on. There's something going on in Saad's room."

I looked at my watch as I waited for Liam. The interview was supposed to take an hour, and it had been nearly that long.

"I'm going in there for Karif now," Liam said. "Rendezvous at the beach in ten minutes."

He shut the radio off. I could hear the crowd yelling out at the front of the hotel and hoped the cops could keep them from entering the grounds.

Gavin and I hurried down through the cool, dimly lit hotel corridors and out into the brilliant sunshine once more. We took a path made of round stones past the pool to the beach and the rental kiosk, where we met a tall, slim Arab man in a crisp white shirt and dark slacks with a radio at his hip. "I am Ilias, and this is François," he said, introducing me to a tanned young Frenchman in silver-rimmed sunglasses with polarized lenses. "He will drive boat for you."

I looked up toward the hotel and saw Liam coming toward us, his hand on Karif's arm. An Arab man followed, arguing.

Gavin started forward, but I grabbed his arm. "In the boat," I said. "Don't fuck things up now. And Gavin?"

"Yeah?"

"No public display of affection until we're out of sight, all right? We don't need anybody with a camera shooting pictures that will show up online before we even make it back to the car."

He grimaced but turned and followed François to a narrow dock where a powerboat was tied up. François jumped in, and Gavin stood on the dock, his arms folded across his chest. It looked like he was imitating the way he'd seen Liam and me stand.

Ilias and I moved up toward Liam and Karif, angling between

them and the man I assumed was Joseph Saad. "That'll be enough," I said to Saad. "In case you haven't figured it out yet, your interview is over."

"This is an outrage!" Saad said. "I was promised a candid conversation with Karif."

"And we were promised you wouldn't say anything about Karif's location," I said. Bouchta and I blocked Saad from following Liam and Karif down the dock. "You called that group out front, didn't you?"

For the first time it appeared Saad heard the shouts of the crowd. They sounded like they were getting closer -- and when I looked up at the hotel, I saw the group of protesters spilling out of the hotel's back door and rushing down that stone path toward us.

I glanced behind me. Liam lifted Karif into the boat, then jumped in after him. Gavin remained on the dock, poised to toss off the mooring line.

The crowd was closing in on us. "Mamhoon!" I shouted, pushing Joseph Saad toward them. "Mamhoon!"

Saad stumbled and fell to one knee. I turned and raced down to the dock, where I jumped into the boat. Gavin threw the line into the boat and jumped in behind me. "*Allez!*" I shouted to François, and he gunned the engine.

Liam stepped up to the front of the boat to talk to François, and I looked back at the beach. Ilias Bouchta had retreated to the kiosk, where he was on his radio. The crowd was yelling at Joseph Saad, and a couple of men had those white stones from the pile at the hotel entrance in their hands.

Behind them I saw a half-dozen Tunisian police officers in their black slacks and light blue shirts waving nightsticks and trying to control the crowd.

François headed straight out to sea, then turned. Within a few minutes, he was pulling up at the public dock at the port. I tossed the car keys to Liam and handed François the last of my cash as Gavin, Karif, and Liam jumped out, Gavin leading the way back to the Land Rover. By the time I scrambled up and raced over to the car, Liam had the boys loaded and the engine going.

I slid into the front seat next to Liam. Gavin and Karif were huddled in the back, Karif shaking and Gavin comforting him. "Good plan," Liam said as we snaked our way out of the parking lot and headed back toward the Villa Palma.

"Why'd you pull Karif out of the interview?" I asked.

"We'll talk about it later," he said.

No one spoke the rest of the way back to the villa. Gavin led Karif upstairs, and Liam and I sat at the kitchen table. Liam pulled the recorder out of his pocket, pressed Rewind, then Play, and we listened to Karif's interview together.

It was all in Arabic, but because both men spoke slowly and carefully, I was able to get most of it. Saad repeated what had happened to Karif since he outed himself, and Karif talked about how he felt. Karif's voice trembled at first, but as he got more comfortable, his voice evened. I figured he'd been through so many interviews in his career, he had to be pretty good at doing them.

Saad seemed particularly interested in the time Karif had spent in Beirut, singing in clubs. I was starting to lose the thread, though, and when Saad asked a question I didn't understand, I looked up at Liam. He flipped the recorder off. "He's asking if Karif knows a man named Ibrahim Fayed," Liam said.

"Why does that name sound familiar?"

"Palestinian politician. Remember how Karif was so interested in that article about the new coalition government there? Fayed is supposed to lead it."

"Why does that matter to Karif? Or Saad?"

"Listen." Liam pressed Play again, and I struggled to translate. Saad's voice became more demanding, Karif's more tentative. When Liam shut the machine off again, he said, "That's when I was talking to you on the radio. Saad is asking Karif to confirm that he had a sexual relationship with Ibrahim Fayed in Beirut."

"Shit."

"My feelings exactly. That's when I went in and pulled Karif out of the interview, and Saad started following us, down the stairs and out to the beach."

The recording broke up after that. I heard bits of Saad's questions, and Liam saying the interview was over.

I looked over Liam's shoulder and saw Gavin standing in the doorway. "Karif wants to talk to you," he said.

17 – CONDITIONAL MOOD

Liam opened a new bottle of Vieux Magon and poured us all glasses. We sat in the living room, the late-afternoon sun streaming in through the sliding-glass doors. Gavin and Karif nestled together on the couch, Liam and me on chairs across from them.

"I meet Ibrahim in Tunis," Karif said. "When I am singing on street. He take me in. Was very good to me." He looked down at his lap.

"Was it a sexual relationship?" I asked gently.

Karif nodded. "But beautiful. Ibrahim, he has much soul."

"He has a wife also." I had done a quick search while Liam opened the wine and the boys settled down. Fayed had been born in Gaza under Israeli control, attended Ben Gurion University, and served in the Israeli army. He'd won a fellowship to study at MIT, where he received his PhD in economics.

He had worked in economic development all around the Arab world, including positions in Tunis, Beirut, and Cairo. A longtime bachelor, he had recently married a young Palestinian woman from a prominent family and lived with her in Ramallah, on the West Bank. The city was the administrative capital of the Palestinian National Authority, and Fayed was a senior official in the government.

The article I scanned touted him as the next prime minister, a man able to pull together the various factions. It wasn't until I got to the bottom of the page that I found it was written by Joseph Saad.

"He always live for politics," Karif said. "Make better for Palestinians."

"He's a saint," Liam said drily. "So you lived with him in Tunis?"

Karif shook his head. "He rent small apartment for me. When he move to Beirut, he ask me come. He say we live together, he get me singing jobs."

His voice wavered, and Gavin took his hand again.

"Did he?" I asked.

Karif nodded. "He get me papers to leave Tunisia and go with him. I live in his apartment with him, but I am singing in clubs, late at night, and Ibrahim, he must sleep. So I am move to small apartment." Karif sat up. "In Beirut, things more free. Ibrahim often come to clubs. Many people know we love each other."

"Did you meet Saad in Beirut?" I asked.

"I am not remembering him, but maybe he is knowing someone from that time."

"When did your relationship with Fayed end?" Liam asked.

"We were two years in Beirut," Karif said. "I am singing in clubs, and Ibrahim is working for big foundation. One day he come to my room and say he move to Cairo." He began to cry. "He say he must leave me. In new job they care more about how he live."

Gavin hugged him. "It's all right, love. That's all in the past."

"Have you been in touch with Fayed since he left you in Beirut?" I asked.

He shook his head. "I stay in Beirut one year more. Then I meet Yaroush."

I raised my eyebrows. "Is Yaroush…"

Karif shook his head. "He is straight. But very good businessman. He say he can make me star. He get me lessons to sing more like pop star. He found song for Eurovision contest, and then I am winning."

"Does Yaroush know about your relationship with Ibrahim Fayed?" Liam asked.

Karif nodded. "But he never tell reporter."

"Someone did" We sat there, drinking our wine and thinking. "We need to call Yaroush," Liam said finally. "He needs to know how things went."

Liam tried to reach Yaroush on the phone but couldn't get him. I fixed dinner, and after we ate, the boys went up to their room together. "The boat was an inspired idea," Liam said as we sat back on the sofa again.

"I didn't want to make Karif go through that crowd," I said. "Once I got that idea in my head, I had to look for ways we could get away from the hotel without going through the front door."

"How does the Palestinian boyfriend fit in?" Liam asked. "You think someone is trying to get to him through Karif?"

"Assuming Karif is telling the truth, they haven't been in contact since the guy dumped him in Beirut."

Our eyes met, and we both said, "Cell phone." While Liam found Karif's phone and identified his carrier, I opened one of those programs we'd collected, which used an anonymous gateway in the Czech Republic to access the records of Tunisie Telecom. We had to pay for the privilege of hacking, which I did using a credit card we'd established for such purposes which could not be traced back to either of us.

It took a couple of minutes for the results to display on the screen. Wary of the iffy Internet service on the island, I immediately downloaded the list to an Excel spreadsheet, and then sorted by country code and city code.

The country code for Tunisia is 216; most of the calls Karif made were within the country itself. The number we had for Yaroush in Rome showed up a couple of times a month, as did a number in Cairo; a quick search showed that was his record company's main number.

More interesting were the calls to country code 970 -- areas in the West Bank and Gaza controlled by the Palestinian National Authority. The city code for the calls was 9722 -- Ramallah, where Ibrahim Fayed now lived.

I had to log back into the anonymous server and pay again to do a cross-match on the owner of the number. His name was Ali Mahfouz, and he lived in Ramallah. "He probably works for the record company," Liam said. "Maybe he's their guy on the ground in the West Bank. Did Karif have any concerts there?"

I checked Karif's Web site for his tour schedule. Sure enough, he had given a concert in Ramallah a few months before. I tried a couple of different ways to hack into the record company's database, but they had firewalls and honey traps and a very good form of password protection. They must have put all those safeguards in place once music pirating reached epic proportions.

I laughed as I gave up and switched to a Google search on Ali Mahfouz. "What's funny?" Liam asked.

"It's easier to hack into a government database than a record company's employee list. Isn't there something wrong with that picture?"

Google provided nearly five thousand results, and for all we knew our guy could be flying under the radar or using an alias for the cell number. Hell, we had a cell phone under the name Bill Thompson that we used when we wanted to remain anonymous. It was impossible to be sure any of the men who popped up in our search was the one Karif had called.

"What now?" I asked. "Should we ask Karif who Ali Mahfouz is?"

"Not yet. We don't want to spook him or piss him off that we're digging into his personal life. This guy could be his fortune-teller or his hairdresser or an old friend he calls when he's depressed."

"How about if we listen to that interview again?" I said. "Maybe there's a clue we missed in something Saad asked."

We went into the kitchen and set the recorder up again. Liam fast-forwarded through most of the conversation. "The question is how much Saad already knew and how much Karif confirmed for him," he said.

When we got to the relevant part, Liam ran the machine in slow mode so we could pick out as much as possible. Saad's language was very elaborate, and it was painstaking for us to dig through the clauses. "That," I said, stopping the machine. "That's the conditional mood, right?"

"You're talking like a teacher, Aidan." It was true; this was the kind of thing I'd gone over endlessly with my ESL students in Philadelphia. "I studied Arabic in the SEALs. I know phrases like 'get your hands up,' not fancy grammar."

"The conditional mood is what you use when you're talking about a hypothetical state of affairs or an uncertain event that's contingent on another set of circumstances," I said. "For example, if Karif and Ibrahim Fayed knew each other, and Karif is gay, then he could have had a sexual relationship with Fayed."

"Is that the way Saad is phrasing it?" Liam asked.

"Play it again." He did, and I found an Arabic-grammar Web site that confirmed what I thought.

"He could have been trying to trip Karif up," I said. "Dancing around the issue and trying to get Karif to confirm something that was only speculation."

"So maybe Saad didn't have any proof to confront Karif with," Liam said. "If he's using this kind of conditional language."

I stood up and started pacing around the kitchen. "I don't think he had any real proof. If he had, he'd have spoken much more simply and clearly. He's a newspaper reporter; he needs to get to the heart of the story. I think he was trying to trick Karif into confirming his hypothesis."

"He might have an anonymous source," Liam said. "Or one that he doesn't completely trust. An actress sued him last year over a story that she had an abortion, and she won. He's probably being very careful."

I returned to Liam's side as he played Karif's response to that hypothetical question. It was slow in coming, but all he said was that Fayed was a friend and mentor who had helped him establish his career in Beirut.

There was nothing more; that was when Liam had interrupted the interview.

Liam turned the machine off and packed it away.

"I don't think he can come out and say Karif had sex with Fayed," I said. "Not based on what I heard. He leaves the paper open for libel, and Fayed is a powerful guy. If I were Saad, I wouldn't want to cross him, at least not without more proof."

"Let's hope Saad thinks like you do," Liam said. "That he learned a lesson from that court case. Otherwise things are only going to get hotter for Karif."

18 – LIKE A WOMAN

Liam yawned. "I'm bushed. I'm going to make one more perimeter check, and then I'm going to bed."

"I'll be there waiting for you."

"Oh, you will, will you?"

I smiled. "You better get moving, stud."

I closed up the downstairs, doing my own check of windows and doors, cleaning up the dirty glasses and plates, and tossing the towels into the washer for Alisa. By the time Liam came in from checking the fence and the garage, I was naked on the four-poster bed, my arms and legs spread out and my dick stiff.

"Now that's something I'm never going to get tired of seeing," Liam said.

He closed the door behind him and stood there looking at me. "You are such a handsome man," he said. "You know that? I look at you sometimes, and I can't get over how sexy you are."

"Yeah, yeah. Enough flattery. Get over here and do something about it."

He laughed. "Pushy bottom. You look like you need someone to tell you who's the boss around here."

"Tell me while you're doing something," I said. "Preferably something that involves my dick."

He stepped over to the bed, then sat on the edge and lifted my right foot into his lap. With the tip of his index finger, he began to trace circles around the sole. I sat up and scooted forward.

His fingers made their way up my leg, teasing their way along my calf and thigh, dancing past my dick to tangle through my pubic hair. I shivered at his touch. "You like that, don't you," he said.

"I'd like it more if you were sucking my dick."

"I suppose you should get a reward for your quick thinking this afternoon," he said, and he lowered his head and took my dick in his mouth. I ran my hands over his back, feeling his muscles through his T-shirt, then closed my eyes and let the sensation take me. He sucked me till I was almost ready to come, then pulled off.

"Liam," I said, my voice strangling.

He smiled and began to play with my nipples. I was so horny I was lifting my body off the bed to get to him. He pretended to be able to walk away at any moment -- but I knew his tricks. He was enjoying the sex as much as I was.

When he put his mouth on my dick again, I blew my load almost immediately, Liam clutching my ass in his hands. When he backed off, licking his lips, I smiled up at him. "You want to get naked, babe?"

He yawned. "I want to go to sleep." He stripped down as I turned on my side. Then he snuggled up to me and we both dozed off.

The phone rang at eight o'clock the next morning. Liam was scouting out the house's perimeter, and the boys were still in bed, so I answered. "English please, Yaroush," I said after a burst of Arabic. "Was the interview in the paper this morning?"

"Yes, and online too," Yaroush said. "It is a major disaster."

My heart did a flip-flop. Had we been wrong about how much Saad knew about Ibrahim Fayed? "Disaster? How?"

"These men, they say Karif is like a woman," Yaroush said, his voice at least one octave higher than normal. "It is one thing to have sex with a man -- but to play the woman's part! No one will want to buy his CDs now. His career is over."

"And Fayed?"

"Fayed?" Yaroush asked.

"What does the article say about Ibrahim Fayed?" I carried the phone over to the coffee table in the living room, where we'd left the laptop the night before.

"There is nothing about Fayed in the article," Yaroush said. "But there are many men who have treated Karif like a woman."

"Enough with the treatment like a woman. You mean he let them fuck him? Or did he just suck their dicks?"

Yaroush took in a quick breath. I guess I had shocked him. "I do not like to talk about such things."

"Liam's outside. As soon as he gets back, we'll read the article and call you."

"I will not be able to work for Karif if there is no money to be made. And the record company will pull his CDs from the stores and ask him to leave the villa."

"Let's take one thing at a time, Yaroush. We'll call you back."

As soon as I hung up, I went out to the pool deck. I saw Liam examining the fence and waved him inside. Then I went back and pulled up the interview at the paper's Web site.

Considering that Saad had flown to Djerba to interview Karif, our client hadn't been quoted very much. Most of the article focused on three men Saad had spoken with in Tunis, all of whom claimed to have had sex with Karif. The story seemed anticlimactic; the world already knew Karif was gay. Who needed additional testimony from three men, listed only by first names?

"Yaroush was right," Liam said, sitting back from the laptop. "This is bad."

"I don't get it. What's so bad about this?"

"The Arab world has a strange relationship with homosexuality," Liam said. "A lot of Arabs will look the other way when it comes to the dominant partner. You know, a guy who lets another guy suck his dick, for example. The guy giving the blowjob has a lot lower status than the guy getting it."

"That's not fair."

"It's what it is. All three of these guys, they say Karif was the passive partner. The bottom. And that makes him look bad."

"It shouldn't matter," I said stubbornly. "Look at us. You're the big, macho one. But you like it when I fuck you, don't you? And you suck me as much as I suck you."

"You and I aren't the ones on trial here. Karif is. And you can't put a Western spin on the story. This is the Arab world, and we have to understand their culture and their prejudices."

"I still don't like it."

"Enough, Aidan. You don't have to like it. You have to live with it. Now go upstairs and wake Karif. He has to see the story before we call Yaroush back."

"Yes, sir," I said, giving him a mock salute.

"And leave the attitude upstairs," he said, swatting my butt as I walked past him.

I knocked on the master-bedroom door; no response. I knocked again, harder, and still got no response.

I opened the door. Both Gavin and Karif were naked, sound asleep. Karif was curled in a fetal position, Gavin sprawled on his back, his beefy dick semihard against his thigh. It reminded me of times when I had woken Liam by taking his dick in my mouth, sucking him to stiffness, bringing him up from his dreams into a very pleasant reality.

An open bottle of lube stood on the bedside table, surrounded by a couple of those yellow condom packets Gavin had brought, empty. The room smelled like sex and sweat.

"Oi," I said, clapping my hands, trying to imitate Gavin's voice. "Wakey, wakey."

Gavin stirred and looked up. "Want to join us, mate?" he asked, scooting aside to make a space between himself and Karif. "There's plenty of room."

"Breakfast downstairs and Karif's interview published online," I said as Karif stirred and stretched on the bed.

Karif sat up. "The interview," he said. "How is it?"

"Come and see for yourself."

They began to get dressed, and I went back downstairs to work on breakfast. Liam sat with them at the kitchen table going over the interview line by line. There were a number of pictures with the interview, mostly publicity shots of Karif. The only recent one was taken as we were boarding the boat to leave the hotel. Karif stood in the stern, with Gavin on one side and Liam on the other. I was still on the dock. The caption read that Karif was under twenty-four-hour protection by hired bodyguards.

"Eejits," Gavin said. "They think I'm one of your bodyguards, love."

"That's better than calling you his boy toy," I said.

"Can a boy have a boy toy?" Liam asked.

"What is boy toy?" Karif asked.

Gavin guffawed. "Guess I am your boy toy, love." He whispered into Karif's ear, and Karif blushed.

I stood up to wash the dishes, and we all heard a loud noise, which could have been a rifle shot, a tree branch cracking, or something hard hitting the roof.

Liam jumped up and hurried to the front door. "Upstairs," I said to Karif and Gavin. "Now." I shepherded them up to the master suite. It faced the ocean, and from the balcony window I could see down to the service drive that led up to the house. A group of about a dozen men stood by the gates, banging and shouting.

A couple of the men were throwing rocks at the house, hitting the garage. Fortunately, the way the house was situated, it was the only part of the property close to the gate; otherwise we'd be under more serious attack.

The noise reminded me of hail back in Philadelphia, the explosive *bang* as each rock hit the metal roof of the garage. Karif was cowering in a fetal position on the bed, while Gavin stood uncertainly next to him. I couldn't tell if he was frightened or defiant.

I pulled the drapes closed. "Stay here until one of us says it's okay," I said. "Gavin, see what you can do to make Karif feel better."

I nodded toward the bed, and Gavin looked at Karif. Then Gavin stood up a little straighter and said, "Will do, mate." He sat down next to Karif and wrapped his arm around the singer, who nestled against him.

Closing the bedroom door behind me, I went into the room I shared with Liam and got the guns from our bags, as well as the binoculars. I joined Liam in the living room, looking slightly downhill at the crowd. "Think it's the same guys who were at the hotel?" Liam asked.

I held the binoculars up and peered through them. "Looks like. I remember that fat guy on the right and the old guy with the grizzled beard."

"Stay here," Liam said. "I'm going to call the police. Holler if anybody breaches the gate."

The men shouted, waved a couple of signs, and threw a few more stones at the garage. Two men left, and I thought that meant the demonstration was winding down. But they returned a few minutes later at the wheel of an ancient Jeep. They nosed the Jeep right up against the gate, and I was worried they were about to try to drive through, but they cut the engine.

I looked back to the house. Should I call Liam? One man jumped onto the hood of the Jeep and grabbed hold of the fence. Another stepped behind him to give him a boost.

I opened the front door and stepped out into my two-handed shooting stance. "*La!*" I shouted, meaning no.

The men stopped for a moment, conferred with each other. Then the first man started climbing again.

Guess that wasn't enough to convince them I was serious. I fired one shot, aiming high. The guy on the bottom backed away, letting his friend fall to the hood of the Jeep. Sweet.

Liam came rushing up behind me as the crowd erupted in more shouting.

"Was that your shot?" Liam demanded.

"Yup. Just a warning."

"No more unless we have to," he said. "The cops are on their way."

We moved forward, Liam going to the left, me to the right. Both of us advanced, ready to fire. We stopped just short of stone-throwing range. Lucky for us, bullets went a lot farther and faster than stones.

We stood like that in a stalemate for at least ten minutes before we heard the police siren approaching.

The crowd tried to disperse, men jumping into the Jeep or running off down the road toward the ocean, but the track up to the house was narrow, and the police blocked the Jeep from exiting. We couldn't hear what went on between the cops and the protesters from where we were.

"Go check on the boys," Liam said. "I'll talk to the cops."

I went inside. The boys had remained in the master bedroom, but from a gentle movement of the curtains at the balcony door, I had a feeling that at least one of them had been watching what happened. Gavin sat on a chair across from the bed, and I wondered why he wasn't next to Karif.

"Why do they want to hurt me?" Karif asked. He was still on the bed, and I could see tearstains on his latte-colored cheeks.

Back in Philadelphia, I volunteered sometimes at the William Way Community Center, counseling gay teenagers about coming-out issues. I remembered one waifishly thin Italian boy from South Philly who was constantly bullied by tougher kids. He had asked me the same question.

I struggled to remember what I'd told him. That life seemed so far in my past. "Some people are frightened by those who are different from them. They may believe that God or Allah or whoever has told them to punish those of us who don't behave the way the majority does."

"That's right bullshit, that is," Gavin said.

"Yeah, I agree," I said. "I used to think that every guy who hated gay men was a closeted queer himself, taking out his repressed feelings on us."

Karif blew his nose and wiped his eyes. "Yes, I am thinking that," he said.

"But living here, in Tunisia, I see things a little different," I said, walking over to the curtains, then pulling them open. "I think a lot of people are scared that their imams have sold them a bill of goods -- that Allah doesn't punish heathens and reward the virtuous. And that makes them want to reach out and hurt people who live with more freedom than they do."

Sunlight streamed back into the room. From the window I saw the police car backing down the drive and Liam walking toward the garage to check for damage.

"Let's go downstairs," I said to the boys. "We're overdue for calling Yaroush back."

They trailed along behind me, not holding hands or even touching each other as they usually did, and I wondered again what had gone on in the bedroom while Liam and I were outside with the mob.

They sat at the kitchen table while I cleaned up. By the time I was finished, Liam joined us there.

"Near as I can tell, the men are from a mosque in Houmt Souk," he said. "The imam got them riled up at the hotel yesterday, then to come out here this morning. The cops talked to them, told them this was private property. They went away, but they might come back."

"Should we leave?" Karif asked.

"Let's call Yaroush." I didn't want to tell them that the record company might kick us out. If they did, and if they declined to keep paying for me and Liam, I didn't know what we'd do. Liam wasn't the type to walk away from someone in trouble and neither was I.

But where could we go? Would the record company charter that plane for us to return to Tunis? Would we have to drive the Land Rover back over the causeway? And once back in Tunis, where would we go? There wasn't room to stash Karif and Gavin in our little house behind the Bar Mamounia. I realized I didn't know where Karif lived or how much money he had in his own name.

Liam turned on the computer and placed the call to Yaroush, turning up the speakers so we could all hear. Karif's manager had calmed down by then, and there were no more threats to pull the plug on Karif or his protection.

"We had an incident this morning." Liam explained about the rock throwers. "The police came out and warned them off. But I'm afraid they may come back."

"I think you are safer on Djerba than back in Tunis," Yaroush said. "But can you keep the house secure against these demonstrators?"

"I need at least two more men," Liam said. "I don't know how fast I can have them in place, so Aidan and I will have to cover the perimeter until then."

"Do what you need," Yaroush said. He paused. "I am at the office of the record company this morning. I am sorry to say there has been another threat."

"Another?" Liam asked. "Similar to the others?"

"I must confess that there have been multiple threats received," Yaroush said. "I thought the ones which threatened death were the most important, and I did not concern myself with the others."

"Others? What kind of others?"

"Someone did not want Karif to speak out further," he said. "He accused Karif of being a blasphemer and said that he would be punished if he spoke again."

"Which he just did, with Joseph Saad," Liam said.

"Yes, I am afraid that was not a good idea," Yaroush said. "The threat which arrived today was very specific. This person is angry that we did not take him more seriously, that we did not listen to him."

"And what does he say now?" Liam asked.

"He does not speak of punishment anymore," Yaroush said. "Now he speaks like the others, of death."

Karif shivered, and Gavin hugged him.

"I looked back at all the threats we received," Yaroush said. "The ones which requested silence are the ones which seem to know the most about Karif and his whereabouts."

"What does that mean?" Liam asked. "Is it someone from the record company? Someone who doesn't want Karif to give any interviews?"

"I will see what I can discover," Yaroush said. Then he asked, "Karif? Are you there?"

Liam handed the microphone to Karif, who took it with a shaking hand. "Yes, Yaroush."

"You stay safe, please," Yaroush said. "We will manage this. Liam and Aidan will take care of you, and you will be singing again soon."

"Thank you," Karif said, and Gavin squeezed his hand as the call ended.

19 – AGE VERIFICATION

I was pleased to see Gavin and Karif back together. All this danger had to be a huge strain on their relationship, and I was worried that Gavin would bolt at any moment, leaving Karif even more despondent.

It was hard for two men to build a relationship in the face of society's lack of respect for their love, and all these pressures and threats had to be complicating their budding romance. It was tough even for Liam and me, when we had to listen to antigay rhetoric spouted by clerics and politicians, or remember not to use endearments in front of clients.

An old boyfriend had compared being gay to swimming in the ocean. "It can be a lot of fun," he'd said. "Playing around in the surf. Falling in love is like dunking yourself under the waves and being totally taken over. But you always have to watch the tides, because they'll sweep you into trouble if you're not careful."

We were all in danger that way, I thought. Karif's death threats. He and Gavin in the first throes of love, where anything can happen. Even Liam and I had to be cautious not to get swamped when trouble arose.

He and I walked into the kitchen together. "Do you want to take the first shift outside, or do you want me to?" I asked.

"The rock throwers won't come back so soon," he said. "I think we have a little leeway here. I'm going to make a call, see what I can work out to get us help."

I went back in the living room as Liam walked off with his cell phone. "Who wants to go for a swim?" I asked the boys.

"Is it safe?" Gavin asked.

I wasn't sure, but I knew we couldn't keep Karif and Gavin inside brooding for too long. "The pool faces the back of the property," I said. "We have a long view, so we'll see anyone approaching that way before they can cause trouble."

They looked at each other. Gavin took Karif's hand again. "Come on, love," he said. "You can't let these eejits run your life."

"Good," I said. "I'll get the towels."

By the time I got outside, they were both naked, splashing around in the pool. I stripped down and dived in with them.

When Liam came back outside, he called me over and said, "I got hold of Ilias Bouchta. He recommended a couple of guys who can watch the gate and the perimeter in shifts. The first one should be here in an hour or so."

He shucked his clothes and dived into the pool with us. The four of us were lounging in the cool water when Liam said, "Karif, who's Ali Mahfouz?"

"I don't know anyone with that name."

Liam looked at me. "You know we're here to protect you," I said to Karif. "But we can't do that unless you are honest with us."

"I am honest," he said. "I do not know that name."

"We checked your phone records," I said. "You've been calling him once or twice a month for the last year."

"I swear to you, I do not know him," Karif said, his voice rising an octave.

"You've been calling his number," I repeated. "In Ramallah."

Karif sucked in a breath and looked pale.

"Who is he, love?" Gavin asked. "Who've you been calling?"

Karif looked down at the water and kicked small eddies with his right foot. "I do not know the name you asked about. I have been calling Ibrahim."

"Ibrahim Fayed?" I asked.

He nodded.

"Your old boyfriend?" Gavin asked. "You still seeing him?"

"No!" Karif said, reaching for Gavin's hand. "I have not seen him in many months. He came to my concert in Cairo, and we talked. That is all! Just talked. He gave me this phone number and told me I could call him if I wanted."

Karif crossed his hands over his chest. "I was very lonely and scared. Ibrahim has always been good to me."

"Did you talk to him about coming out?" I asked.

"Yes. He did not think it was a good idea." He began to cry. "He was right."

Gavin wrapped him in a hug. "Could Ali Mahfouz be another name that Ibrahim uses when he wants to be anonymous?" I asked. I saw confusion on Karif's face, so I clarified. "Maybe that's the name he gives to men he has sex with?"

"No, no," Karif said. "Ibrahim is very honest man."

"Then who is Ali?"

Karif's mouth opened, and then he smiled. "Now I am remembering. Ibrahim tell me he has assistant, Ali. I am not knowing his last name. But must be."

That was one small mystery cleared up. We stayed in the pool, or lounging beside it, for a few hours. Everybody covered up when Alisa came to clean; as soon as she finished upstairs, the boys retreated up to Karif's bedroom.

I decided we'd eat in that night and called Hakim, the caretaker, and gave him a grocery list. It was probably better that none of us left the villa, at least not for a day or two.

My first serious boyfriend was a senior I met at the start of my junior year in college. We dated for most of the year, until he announced he was moving to California after graduation. I had obsessed about him for years afterward, looking him up in phone books and computer databases. I never spoke to him after his graduation, but I liked the idea of knowing where he was, fantasizing that he'd realize his mistake and come back to me.

I had a feeling that there was more to Karif's connection to Ibrahim Fayed than he was saying. I thought maybe if I put together a timeline, something might show up. Late in the afternoon, a guy showed up to watch the gate for us, and Liam went outside to talk to him.

Karif and Gavin came downstairs, and I asked Karif if I could see his passport. "I want to write out when the things you told us about happened," I said. "Maybe that will help us figure out how Joseph Saad found out about you and Fayed."

Karif shrugged but brought his passport downstairs for me. I looked at it, marking down the dates when he had lived in Beirut, when he had returned to Tunis. I looked at the picture and compared it to the young man in front of me. "I have to say, you don't look twenty-five," I said, handing it back to him.

"I am not," Karif said. "I have twenty-three. Or I will next month."

"Give me the passport back, please." I looked at it. "This says you were born in 1985. That makes you almost twenty-five."

Karif shook his head again. "Ibrahim is changing my birth when applying for paperwork. Otherwise I am being too young to leave with him."

I looked at the dates I'd written down. "This passport was issued in 2003, right after your birthday. You're saying you weren't eighteen then?"

He counted on his fingers. "Sixteen."

"And you were how old when you met Ibrahim Fayed?"

He looked down at his lap. "Nothing to be ashamed of," Gavin said. "I done much worse myself at that age."

"I am fourteen," Karif said.

I sat back in my chair and tried to remember the questions Saad had asked, but I couldn't be sure because my Arabic was still so limited. "Did Saad ask you anything about how old you were?"

Karif shook his head.

"Well, that's one good thing." I sat there with them, sipping wine, until Liam returned. "We figured out something while you were gone." I sketched out the timetable for Liam.

I was surprised to see how angry Liam became as I spelled out the details. "You mean to tell me you were fourteen years old when you started having sex with this man?" he demanded of Karif, who began to cry again.

"Oi, mate, no need for that one," Gavin said. He took Karif's hand.

Liam shook his head. "Do you understand what would happen to Fayed's career if this came out? Not just that he had an affair with a man -- but that he had one with a fourteen-year-old boy?"

"You think he would want Karif dead?" Gavin asked in a small voice.

"No," Karif said. "Ibrahim love me. He never want to hurt me."

The three of us looked at him. Karif looked from me to Liam, then to Gavin, and he began sobbing. Gavin put his arm around him. "Come on, love," he said. "Let's get you upstairs."

Liam and I stayed in the living room as Gavin led Karif up to their bedroom.

I stood up. "Let's see what else we can find out about Ibrahim Fayed."

Liam followed me back to the kitchen, where we began using every resource at our disposal to research Ibrahim Fayed. As a public figure, there was a lot about him online, mostly political stuff. He was often quoted in news stories, and the press had begun paying attention as he rose in the Palestinian National Authority.

What we wanted was buried much deeper, though. I wanted to

know if there had been any rumors about his sexuality, if he'd ever been arrested. A man who was sexually involved with one fourteen-year-old boy most likely had been interested in others.

I didn't find more than vague innuendo. One of Fayed's political opponents had said a few things about him a couple of years before, which I had a feeling had led to his marriage. There was an indication that he and his young wife lived separately -- she spent most of her time in an apartment in a compound owned by her family, while he had his own small house and traveled frequently.

Liam took over, using the Voice over IP software to make a few calls, nosing around with contacts he had in Beirut and Cairo while I found a movie on the satellite that all four of us could agree on, a gay romantic comedy about two guys in Los Angeles fumbling toward love.

We ate dinner without talking much and then moved into the living room for the movie. "I want go to Los Angeles," Karif said when the ending credits were rolling. "Yaroush is thinking I sing there."

"You will," Gavin said. "You and me, love, we're going to see the world. I'm going to take care of you, and you're going to sing your heart out."

The two of them went upstairs, and there was some muted banging of the furniture. Liam checked in with the guard outside, and then we went upstairs ourselves.

As Liam stripped and got into bed, I pulled off my T-shirt and shorts. I realized he'd been too quiet ever since the movie ended.

"You okay?" I asked, shimmying out of my boxers and then sliding into bed next to him.

He crossed his arms over his chest. "I hate that this fucker took advantage of Karif when he was still a kid."

"Karif is not exactly a fragile flower. My guess is that fooling around with Ibrahim Fayed was a business transaction for him, despite the crocodile tears."

"How old were you?" Liam asked quietly. "Your first time?"

Uh-oh. I didn't like that tone or the question. But I took a deep breath and said, "I was a late bloomer. I was nineteen, a sophomore in college."

"Who was he?"

"He was actually younger than I was. I had a part-time job as an usher at the campus theater, and he was a kid in the glee club. I was closing up the theater after one of their performances, and he was in the bathroom, jerking off, when I went in to turn the lights off."

Liam shifted so he was resting his head on my chest, and I wrapped an arm around him. "He was sitting on the toilet with the stall door open, and he was as surprised as I was when I saw him there." I laughed at the memory. "I saw his hand on his dick, and he looked up at me and smiled. And I just knew. I went down on my knees, and he stuffed his dick in my mouth. The rest is history, as they say."

I rubbed my hand over his shoulder. "How about you?"

"I was fourteen," he said. "Just like Karif."

"Wow. You want to tell me about it?"

"I played basketball then. This youth league out of New Brunswick."

Liam grew up in New Jersey, not far from where I did, but we hadn't talked much about those years. "Uh-huh," I said.

"This older guy, an assistant at Seton Hall, gave up his free time to coach us. Most of the kids were from the inner city, didn't have dads, and he took an interest in everybody. My dad was a drunk, you know, so he wasn't the type to get out and toss a ball around with me. I really loved that league."

"Did he…" I asked.

"Not him," he said. "He always had these assistants who'd come and go, often guys who had been good college ballplayers but not good enough for the NBA. They'd volunteer with him for a few months or a year to get some coaching experience, so they could get jobs. This one guy named Larry had played in Europe for a couple of seasons, but then he blew out his knee and had to come home."

Liam shifted around so that he was lying on his back with my arm under his head. "Larry was great. He was so smart, and he always had good advice. When we made it into a regional tournament, Coach couldn't go with us because he had a game of his own, so Larry took us."

Outside, the wind picked up, buffeting the house with sand and then rain. "We had to stay overnight in Camden," Liam said, sitting up. "We didn't have a lot of money for motel rooms, so we had to double up. I ended up in a room with Larry."

The house creaked in the wind. "We got the last room, with a king-size bed. Larry even made a joke about it, that I'd better keep my hands to myself. I was mortified -- how did he know what I wanted? But when he came out of the bathroom, he was naked, and I got a major boner. You could see it jamming against my pants."

He laughed, but there was no humor in the sound. "Funny how when I think about that time, it's like I'm still fourteen. He said I ought to strip down, that it was just like we were in a locker room. I was so scared, I was shaking. That he knew I had a hard-on, that he knew what I was, that he'd tell the whole team and I'd get kicked off."

I didn't say anything, just sat up, wrapped my arms around my knees and kept listening.

"He came over and pulled my T-shirt off over my head. He said that he wouldn't bite -- unless I wanted him to."

"Poor baby," I said, shifting closer.

"Dumb joke, right? I giggled, and he put his arm around me and kissed me on the mouth. It was the first time anybody ever kissed me like that."

"Were you as big as you are now, back then?" I asked.

"Almost this tall, but skinny. I didn't get into bodybuilding till the next year." He was quiet for a while, staring off into space. "Now that I think about it, he didn't have that huge a dick, but it seemed pretty big back then. I'd never seen another guy hard, certainly not a man. He reached down and put my hand on it, and it was so warm and, you know, vital. Like he was letting me into some secret part of himself."

He turned to look at me. "Then he pulled my hand off, and he spit into my palm. I was grossed out -- but then he put my hand back on his dick, and I knew what he wanted. He kept on kissing me as I started to jerk him off."

"You don't have to tell me all this if you don't want to," I said.

"I want to. I want you to understand. I jerked him for a while, and then he pulled down my shorts and got on his knees and blew me. He wanted me to blow him too, but I was freaked out. So I just jerked him some more, and he came. And then he got into the bed and went to sleep."

"What did you do?"

"I curled up on the floor. I pulled the comforter over me, but I never went to sleep."

"You can sleep here with me. I'll protect you."

He leaned over and kissed me. "I know you will."

20 – KITE SURFING

We were eating breakfast Sunday morning when the doorbell rang. "What the fuck?" Liam asked, pushing his chair back from the table. "How did somebody get past Bakri out front?" We had three men outside, each on an eight-hour shift. Bakri was our daytime guard, Mudar took over in the afternoon, and Luqman kept watch during the night.

After the stone-throwing incident the day before, we'd decided to keep our guns with us or nearby at all times. Liam pulled his from its holster as I shepherded Gavin and Karif to the laundry room, the safest spot on the first floor. The door locked from the inside, and I told them to stay there until we knew who was at the door.

I remained a few paces behind Liam as he went to the front door and peered through the peephole. "It's all right," he said. "It's Ilias Bouchta."

Ilias noticed Liam holstering his gun as Liam opened the door. "I am sorry to surprise you," he said. "Bakri knows me, of course, and he opened the gate. We did not realize it would upset you." He smiled. "But I am glad to see you are prepared." He was wearing his hotel uniform, and I wondered if he ever got a day off.

I got Karif and Gavin from the laundry room, and we all went back to the breakfast table, where Ilias accepted my offer of a glass of orange juice. "I was angry that these protesters disturbed guests at my hotel," he said, "so I began to ask some questions. I thought you would be interested in the answers I found."

He sipped his juice. "The men who protested at the hotel and here at your villa came from the mosque in Houmt Souk. This morning I spoke to the imam there. He told me that he was asked to organize the protest by another imam, a very powerful one from Cairo. He had no choice but to agree."

"Who is that?" Liam asked.

"His name is Hassen Ben Chedi," Ilias said.

Karif caught his breath, and Liam and I exchanged looks. "You know this man?" Ilias asked.

"He's the one who put the fatwa out against Karif," I said.

"Why does this imam harbor such a hatred for you?" Ilias asked Karif. "Do you know him?"

Karif shook his head. "I never hear his name before he make the fatwa."

"This man is a powerful enemy," Ilias said. "He is a very important imam with much influence."

We thanked Ilias for his help, and he went back to work. While Gavin and Karif went swimming and I cleaned up, Liam Googled Hassen Ben Chedi. "What did you find?" I asked, joining him in the living room.

He shrugged. "Nothing much. Ilias is right; he's a powerful man. But I can't figure out why he cares so much about Karif. I checked; he has issued other fatwas, but never about homosexuality."

"I have an idea." I swiveled the laptop around to face me and searched for *Hassen Ben Chedi* and *Ali Mahfouz*.

No results matched my search terms. Then I tried *Hassen Ben Chedi* and *Ibrahim Fayed*.

There were nearly a hundred hits. I shifted the screen so that Liam could see. "I think we have our connection," I said.

We started going through the results. Both Ibrahim Fayed and the imam had served on several important committees and had been guests at many of the same charitable and political events.

"Ideas?" Liam asked.

"I think it's safe to assume Hassen Ben Chedi knows there is a connection between Ibrahim and Karif. From there we can only speculate why Ben Chedi has it in for Karif."

"Maybe Fayed is angry," Liam suggested. "He asked the imam to issue the fatwa as a way to get back at Karif."

"Angry about what? Karif has the right to come out of the closet if he wants."

Liam got up and started pacing around the living room. "Fayed molested Karif when he was fourteen. If that news gets out, it destroys Fayed's career."

"Or Ben Chedi wants something from Fayed, and he's threatening to get Karif killed if Fayed doesn't go along."

"That's a possibility," Liam said. "But that means Ben Chedi knows about the relationship between Karif and Fayed. Do you think Ibrahim would spread that around?"

"Maybe Ben Chedi is his spiritual advisor. Like a confessor. Don't you tell your priest all your sins?"

"I don't have a priest, and I don't believe in sin," Liam said.

"The only way we're going to figure this out is to have Karif call that phone number again and ask his ex a few questions."

Karif and Gavin were still wet, lying on lounge chairs with their eyes closed. When we opened the sliding-glass doors, both of them sat up.

Liam took the chair next to Karif. "When was the last time you spoke to Ibrahim Fayed?" he asked.

"It was day or two before I make announcement," Karif said. "He is not happy. He warn me nothing good come from such deciding."

"That was very selfish of him," I said.

"He say he not want to talk to me again," Karif said in a small voice.

"We need you to call him," Liam said. "He knows this imam, the one who issued the fatwa. It's possible that the imam did it at his request."

"No! This could not be."

"It's one of the possibilities," I said gently. "There could be many others. But we will only know if you speak to Ibrahim."

"I don't think it's a good idea," Gavin said, his arms crossed against his chest. "The man has already said he doesn't want to talk to Karif. I say to hell with him."

"Karif?" I asked.

He looked so unhappy, I wanted to go over and put my arm around him. His ex might be behind the plot to kill him, and his new boyfriend was jealous. Jealousy, though, was the least of his problems at the moment.

"Gavin," I said. "If you really want Karif to be safe, you'll help us persuade him to make that call." I pursed my lips and stared at him.

Years of teaching had helped me perfect that look. I'd stared down hundreds of students over the years, from the Guatemalan who insisted he had no accent, to the Haitian woman who thought she could get a better grade by making a pass at me, to the dozens who didn't think they had to do their homework.

I could see the emotions warring on Gavin's face, and I felt sorry for him. He did seem to love Karif, beyond their obvious infatuation and lust. And he'd already decided he was going to be Karif's protector. His brain told him this was the right way to go, and eventually it overruled everything else.

"You need to do it, love," he said, reaching out for Karif's hand.

Karif kept his hands to himself for a moment, then finally took Gavin's. "All right," he said.

Gavin brought down Karif's cell phone from the bedroom, and Karif dialed the number. We all heard the phone ring, and then the voice mail picked up. "Ibrahim," Karif said in a voice so soft and low I was afraid it wouldn't register. I was able to translate most of his Arabic as he spoke; the gist was that Karif needed to speak with him, that he'd been told Ibrahim knew the imam who had issued the fatwa. "Do you hate me, Ibrahim?" he asked, choking back tears. Then he disconnected the call.

Gavin enveloped him in a hug, and Liam and I left them out by the pool.

The news about Ibrahim's relationship to the imam -- and being cooped up in the villa -- was taking a toll on Karif. By lunchtime he wasn't speaking at all and didn't want Gavin touching him.

It was Sunday, Alisa's day off, so after we ate, I took it upon myself to clean up the master bedroom while the boys were out at the pool. Standing at the balcony overlooking the ocean, I saw the white sails of a kite surfer sailing across the ocean.

I went downstairs and found Liam at the computer. "What about taking Gavin and Karif out for some kite surfing lessons?" I asked. "Ilias could set it up at the Hotel Grand Djerba. I think the boys need something to cheer them up."

"Are you nuts?" he asked.

"No. But you've always said it's our responsibility to keep the client happy as well as safe, right?"

"But kite surfing?"

"It'll be tough; it'll force them to concentrate and it'll tire them out. Sounds like just what they need."

"Fine. Call Ilias and see what he can set up."

Ilias was happy to organize a private lesson, and an hour later we were on our way back into Houmt Souk. Karif still wasn't talking or responding to any of Gavin's overtures, but he was allowing himself to be pulled along.

Our instructor was François, the Frenchman who had piloted the boat we used to escape the protestors. We began with a video lecture, showing us the different kinds of kites and demonstrating how they harnessed the wind. "The surf is a dangerous partner," the narrator intoned. "You must be sure to pay attention to its moods."

That was all we needed, I thought. More mood swings. In my relationship with Liam, I was generally content to take the secondary role, deferring to his experience, his strength, his bossy personality. But sometimes I rebelled, and we fought.

The up-and-down nature of the threats against Karif made things even tougher. Sometimes it seemed like we were all on vacation together at the villa, happily skinny-dipping and making love with our respective partners. And then other times, we were reminded of our dangerous situation.

Perhaps it hadn't been a good idea to suggest an activity that added another layer of danger to what was already a difficult assignment. Adding the unpredictable surf as another antagonist didn't make things any easier.

But then François demonstrated how to get into the wet suits, the harness, and the helmet, and we all had a couple of good laughs at the awkwardness. By the time we went outside, Karif had started to show some interest.

François offered to hook him up first, but Karif said, "I watch Gavin."

Gavin was like an eager puppy. He fell into the water a couple of times, but once he got the hang of it, he took off across the bay with a whoop. Karif was so caught up in watching him that he didn't have time to worry or feel bad about Ibrahim and the possibility that his ex-boyfriend was behind the fatwa on him.

Karif went next, and then he and Gavin sat on the sand and laughed as Liam fumbled through his start. Watching him, though, I began to think this wasn't as good an idea as I thought. If Liam had trouble keeping the kite downwind and then gaining his balance once he slipped his feet into the straps on the board, how was I going to manage?

Liam took off and began soaring across the beachfront, whooping. He suddenly seemed to sink into the water, and then the kite turned, and he rose up again.

"Is okay," Karif said, seeing me watch. "Is just turning."

By the time Liam returned, I was determined not to take my turn. When François motioned me to take the handle of the kite, I shook my head. "Go on, Aidan," Liam said, peeling off his vest. "It's fun."

"The boys are tired," I said. "Let's go back to the villa and have dinner."

"No, no," Gavin and Karif chorused. "You go."

I shook my head again. The boys started chanting, "Ai-dan, Ai-dan," and Liam grabbed my arm.

"You've got to do this," he said, dragging me toward where François stood. "This was all your idea."

"I don't want to." I planted my feet in the sand and crossed my arms.

"Why not? Why the sudden change?"

I looked down at the sand. "I'm scared."

When I looked up, there was confusion in Liam's eyes. "Scared?

Why? We've all done it, and we're fine. You have a harness. Nothing can happen."

"You really don't know? Sometimes I think you don't understand me at all."

"Aidan. Stop being a child and put the damn harness on."

"I'm not being a child. What if I can't do it? What if I look like a fool and you realize I'm not cut out to be a bodyguard at all?"

Liam's eyes opened wider, and then he smiled. "Being a bodyguard has nothing to do with whether you can kite surf or not," he said. "You've already shown me in a hundred ways that you're smart enough and strong enough and sharp enough to handle anything this job throws at us."

He wrapped his arm around my shoulder, and I leaned into him. "This isn't about proving anything. It's about having fun. Give it a try. I know you, and I think you'll like it."

I blew out a big breath. "Fine. But if you laugh at me, I'm going to bite your penis off the next time I have it in my mouth."

"Deal," he said, pushing me toward François.

I sat on the sand first, controlling the kite with the navigation bar, and it brought back memories of flying kites back in New Jersey. All too quickly, though, François had me in the water, and then he gave me the bar and I took off.

"Oh my God!" I shouted, as the wind took hold of me and I lifted off the ground. Everything I'd learned from the video and listening to François went out of my head, and I felt a moment of pure panic. But then I turned the bar a little and the kite changed direction, and I felt like I could handle this. By the time I landed, I was just as exhilarated as Liam and the boys.

The kite surfing lifted Karif's and Gavin's spirits and tired them out. They were ravenously hungry for dinner, which I threw together back at the house.

We were just finishing when Karif's cell phone rang. "Is Ibrahim," he said. "Is ring tone I make for him."

He didn't move to get up, though. I nodded to Gavin, who scrambled up, got the phone from the living room, and brought it to Karif. "Go on, love," Gavin said. "You've got to get this out."

Karif took the phone and flipped it open. "Ibrahim?" he said in a small voice.

The three of us sat and watched as Karif listened for a long time. Finally he told Ibrahim to hold on and turned to us. "He is knowing this man, this imam, but he is not asking for fatwa."

"That's good," I said. "Can he get the imam to call it off?"

"He say he call the imam," Karif said. He stood up and took the phone with him out to the pool deck.

Gavin looked stricken. "Don't worry, Gavin," I said. "Karif's not going back to him."

"You don't know that," he said, looking down at the table.

"I know. There's no going back once you come out of the closet. Ibrahim's married, and he's made it clear that his political career is more important to him than Karif."

Gavin looked up.

"If I were you, I'd wait until he finishes that call, then go outside with him."

Gavin stood up, smiled, and walked out to the living room.

"How'd you get so smart?" Liam asked me, smiling.

"Years of practice. Dating unavailable guys, listening to other guys complain about their problems."

"You believe that?" Liam asked. "About not being able to go back in the closet after you come out?"

I started clearing the table. "Coming out is a process," I said. "You don't just wake up one day, say 'I'm here; I'm queer,' and that's it. You start out by admitting to yourself. Then you move on to the important people in your life. If you're a public figure, like Karif, you can either get dragged out unwillingly, make a statement, or if you're very lucky, let it happen without anyone making a big deal."

I looked over at him. "But once you take that first step, and you admit it to yourself -- you can't go back from that unless you're ready to start lying."

Liam nodded, then pulled on his reading glasses and picked up a newspaper we had bought at the hotel. But I had the feeling that wasn't the end of the conversation.

21 – SMALL EXPLOSIONS

Karif and Gavin stayed outside for a while; then we all watched another movie together. We'd just turned off the TV, about eleven, when we heard a series of shots or small explosions coming from outside.

I rushed Karif and Gavin into the laundry room and killed the lights as Liam grabbed the flashlight and his gun and went to the front window. We had been keeping those curtains closed in case anyone else came up to the gate. When I came into the living room again, I found him standing at the side of the window, the curtains ticked away just an inch so he could see out.

He raised the radio and said in Arabic, "Luqman. You there?"

We stood there until Luqman's voice came out of the radio. "Fireworks, boss," he said, in English. "Down by the beach."

"Could be a distraction," Liam told him. "Stay there. I'm coming down."

He handed the radio to me. "You stay with the boys. I'll meet up with Luqman and give you the all clear."

"Be careful." I leaned up and kissed his cheek, rough with the day's stubble, as I took the radio from him.

I went back to the laundry room, where the boys sat on the floor, Gavin with his arm around Karif. "Looks like it's nothing," I said. "Just fireworks by the beach. But Liam's going out to check."

"I am living life like this forever?" Karif asked. "Afraid of every sound?"

I didn't know how to answer that. I was pretty sure that the fuss over his coming out would fade as soon as something new came up. But I also knew that Salman Rushdie, the author who'd been subject to a death-threat fatwa, had lived under police guard for years and probably still started at any sudden noise.

"We're taking this one day at a time, all right?" I said to Karif. "Every day we get through without trouble is a good one."

"Aidan?"

Liam's voice boomed through the radio and bounced off the walls of the narrow laundry room. I stood up and walked out to the hallway. "Here," I said.

"Looks like Luqman was right. Some kind of festival down by the beach. I'm going to stay out here with him for a while, though, just to be sure no one is using that as a distraction. You get the boys up to bed."

"All right."

I sent Karif and Gavin upstairs, then waited for Liam to come back in, keeping my gun, my flashlight, and the radio handy. I was relieved when he walked in. "At least we're keeping on our toes," he said. I could see he was tired; his body sagged in small ways I had come to recognize. His face was smudged with dirt, and he had a long scratch down his arm.

"What were you doing?" I asked, standing up to go upstairs with him.

"Luqman and I crawled around, making sure no one had

sabotaged the wall. I'm going to jump in the shower before bed." He walked ahead of me into the bedroom and began shedding his clothes, and the last thing I saw as he disappeared behind the bathroom door was his round ass cheeks, nearly as tan as the rest of him now that we'd been spending so much time sunbathing nude by the pool.

I wondered if he wanted company in the shower. We both liked our personal space sometimes, as much as we enjoyed fooling around and making love. He was tired, and maybe he did just want to get cleaned up before bed.

I decided to think with the little head rather than the big one. And the little head knew exactly what I should do. I stripped down, tossed my clothes aside for the laundry, and stepped into the bathroom. I could see Liam lathering up behind the clouded glass door. I opened it and looked inside.

"You coming in?" he asked.

That was all the welcome I needed. I stepped in, closed the door behind me, and embraced him. He leaned down to kiss me, and his body relaxed. We kissed under the spray for a couple of minutes. His mouth was almost desperate for mine, his lips pressing hard, his tongue snaking out. He wrapped his arms around me and pulled me tight to him, his brawny, muscular body so close to mine. The soapsuds began running down my chest and legs as my dick swelled against his thigh, his dick pressing into my belly.

I began massaging his shoulders as we continued to kiss. He was so tense, and I couldn't blame him. It had been a hell of a week since we'd gotten the first call from Yaroush.

My hands lathered Liam's back, straying down to his ass. I massaged the soap into his cheeks and his crack, even fingering my way to his hole. He groaned as I did that, leaning his head back so the water cascaded over his face.

I ran the soap over his broad pecs, rubbing the edge of the bar against his nipples, then swiped it down his chest, over his six-pack abs to his groin. I lathered my hands up good and used them to cover his dick and bush with suds.

He stepped away from the direct spray, so his dick and groin stayed soapy, and he took the bar of soap from me and rubbed it over my chest. He took a handful of suds and began stroking my dick. I shivered as my body yielded to his touch.

Liam put the soap aside and pulled my body to his. We kissed once more, rubbing together. He grabbed my ass and pressed me to him, and our dicks slithered against each other in a growing momentum. I was having trouble catching my breath between the steam in the shower and the way my mouth was constantly pressed against Liam's.

He arched his back and pressed down even harder on my mouth as his dick spurted come. He wrapped his leg around mine, sliding his thigh against my dick, and I gave in to the sensation, yelping as the orgasm overtook me.

We held on to each other for a while, swaying together as the water cascaded over us. I finally backed away, rinsed away the last of the soapsuds, and poured shampoo into my hands. "Lean backward,"

I said to Liam as I rubbed my hands together to generate a lather.

I shampooed his hair, then my own, and we stepped out into the steamy bathroom together. We wrapped ourselves in oversize Turkish towels and dried off. We were both exhausted, and we stumbled to the bed, falling damply together and pulling the covers over us.

The next morning when I woke up, Liam was already awake, sitting next to me in bed with the laptop computer. "What's up?" I asked, yawning.

"Checking e-mail," he said. "I don't know where Yaroush is, but I need to get hold of him and talk about what's been happening. Even with the extra security at the gate, I don't think we can stay here in Djerba anymore. Those fireworks last night were a wake-up call. We're just not secure enough here to stand up to someone who is determined to hurt Karif. We could barely manage having the local mosque organize some rock throwing."

"What about more security?" I asked. "Additional patrols outside?"

"I don't think extra security will help. We need to move Karif to a more secure location."

"Where could we go?"

"That's what I want to talk to Yaroush about. Maybe the record company has a house somewhere else, a city like Cairo or Rome or London."

"We have to be realistic. See what the record company is willing to pay for. Remember how Yaroush said if Karif's records stop selling, the money dries up."

"We're not abandoning Karif."

I got out of bed, stretching. Liam's clothes were still strewn on the floor where he had dropped them the night before, and reflexively I began picking them up. "And who's going to support us if we're not getting paid?" I asked.

"I'm concentrating," Liam said, hunched over the laptop composing his e-mail to Yaroush.

"God forbid you should multitask. Or pick up your own dirty clothes."

"Shut up, Aidan. I told you, I'm working."

"Like you're the only one who ever does that." He looked up and glared at me. "Fine. I'm going downstairs to start breakfast."

He went back to his e-mail, and I pulled on shorts and a T-shirt. By the time he and the boys came downstairs. I had breakfast ready for everyone. Liam kissed my forehead as he walked past me. "Sorry for yelling at you," he said.

"'S okay," I said. "We're all tense."

"I am not knowing I am putting so much people in danger when I make announcement," Karif said, sitting at the kitchen table.

"You have a right to live your life," Gavin said, joining him and squeezing his hand.

"I am not being sure," Karif said. "I am thinking I must go somewhere, like America. Live in cave or underground."

"It's not that easy," Liam said. "First of all, we thought you'd be safe here at the villa. But someone knew exactly where you were and told Joseph Saad and that imam in Cairo who orchestrated the demonstrations."

After breakfast Liam tried to phone Yaroush, but the call went direct to voice mail. "Who wants to go swimming?" I asked, trying to brighten the heavy mood.

"No swimming," Liam said. "I want everyone to stay inside for a while. Just like you don't go in the ocean when there are heavy currents, you stay indoors when people are throwing rocks at you."

I was getting tired of Liam making all the decisions without consulting me, but I held back. No arguing in front of the client.

"Come on, love. Let's watch some telly," Gavin said, pulling Karif to the living room.

"Let's stay in for dinner," Liam said in a low voice when they were gone. "Can you throw something together?"

"I can do more than throw something together. I'm a gourmet cook, remember?"

"Can you do it with a little less attitude?"

I realized I was holding my body tense, and relaxed. "I'm letting this get to me too much, aren't I?"

"We'll get through it. Just try and stay calm and focused."

While Liam sat at the kitchen table with the laptop, I searched through the cabinets and the refrigerator to see what we had and what I would need Hakim to bring us. After I called him with our grocery list, I baked a chocolate cake, trying not to bang the pans too loudly, offering a spoonful of frosting to Liam.

"You're going to make us all fat," he said, but he took the spoon

198 | NEIL S. PLAKCY

from me and licked it clean.

As I was finishing, Karif said he had a headache and went upstairs to take a nap. Gavin asked if he could go out for a walk. "Don't see why not," Liam said. "I'll call Bakri at the gate and tell him you're going."

After Gavin walked out the front door, Liam said, "Think he's coming back?"

"I hope so. It'll break Karif's heart if he runs off. Plus he didn't take his bag or any of his clothes."

"If he's working with whoever is after Karif, that won't matter to him."

"But if he wanted to hurt Karif, he's had so many opportunities," I said.

"There's something about him I just don't trust," Liam said. "There's something he's hiding. I just haven't figured it out yet."

I walked to the front window and watched Gavin shuffle down the drive, kicking stones. His head was bowed, and he was the picture of dejection. Bakri let him out the gate, and he disappeared in the grove of olive trees between us and the ocean road.

22 – RELIEF

The oven timer went off, and I pulled the cake layers out, then tipped them out of their pans to cool. Alisa arrived to clean, bringing our groceries, and I asked her to skip vacuuming or cleaning the boys' room. Gavin still had not returned by the time I had made frosting for the cake, applied it to the cooling layers, and piped tiny flowers on the top.

The knock at the front door surprised us. Liam looked up from the laptop, and I knew he was worried about Bakri -- how had someone gotten past him? Was it Ilias Bouchta again? Who else knew we were at the villa?

Liam pulled his gun out of his holster and moved to the front door. He looked out the peephole, and I could see his body relax. "It's Gavin," he said.

Gavin looked dirty and sweaty, though nowhere near as bad as he had when I first saw him getting that blowjob from Karif in the alley in Houmt Souk. "Had to clear my head some." He smiled. "Any lunch left?"

I made up a couple of sandwiches on pita bread. "Why don't you take this upstairs, see if you can get Karif to eat something?"

"You are such a mom," Liam said when he'd gone.

"Speaking of which." I remembered our dog, how we had left her with the bartender at the Bar Mamounia. "Have you spoken to Fadi? How is Hayam?"

"She's fine. You know that dog. She gets along with everyone."

When Karif and Gavin came downstairs, Gavin asked, "Still no swimming?"

"Sorry," Liam said. Just then the house phone rang. Liam answered; I deciphered his Arabic to figure out that he was speaking to Bakri at the gate. When he hung up, he said, "Yaroush is here."

Karif smiled broadly. "Is wonderful," he said, jumping up. He headed to the front door. "Yaroush know what to do." Liam followed him.

Gavin remained on the sofa, his face guarded. "Yaroush is a nice guy," I said to him. "He wants what's best for Karif."

"But what if that's not me?" Gavin asked.

"We'll cross that bridge when we come to it." I stood up. "Come on; let's introduce you."

Yaroush was all smiles. "I have wonderful news," he said as soon as he walked in the front door, carrying a small briefcase. "I had to come here and tell you myself." He looked like he had been traveling for a while; his gray curls were tousled and his suit jacket wrinkled.

"First you meet Gavin," Karif said, taking Yaroush by the arm and leading him across the room. Liam followed carrying Yaroush's overnight bag. "Gavin is being my new boyfriend," Karif said, smiling broadly. "Is wonderful man!"

Gavin stuck his hand out shyly. "Karif has told me a lot about you," he said. "Thank you very much for keeping him safe."

Yaroush eyed him but took his hand and shook it. "Well, all this will change now. Come, come, I have much to tell you."

We sat in the living room. "I read your e-mail," he said to Liam. "I am glad you have been able to keep Karif safe, and I understand your concerns. But now things are changing." He smiled. "I have discovered how information was being supplied to the press. There is a secretary at the record company, Atifa Mohammed. Do you remember her, Karif? A very young woman?"

"Yes. She is wanting date me before I am out of closet. She not accept my decline."

"She is not a good woman," Yaroush said. "She has been telling private information about you to other people. For money."

"What kind of people?" Liam asked.

"The newspaper columnist," Yaroush said. "The imam Hassen Ben Chedi."

"That's the one that put the fatwa on you?" Gavin asked Karif.

"What awful person!" Karif said. "Because I am not being her boyfriend!"

"I'm sure the money had something to do with it too," Yaroush said.

"That explains how Saad knew where you were and how the imam at the mosque in Houmt Souk was able to organize the crowd at the hotel and then at the front gate," Liam said.

"But that is all over with," Yaroush said. "She has been fired. This morning. The president of the record company agreed not to prosecute her if she would go away quietly."

"What does this mean for Karif now?" I asked.

"I think he must stay under protection for a few more days," Yaroush said. "Just to be careful. And then this will all be past us."

He opened his briefcase. "I have even more news." He pulled a sheet of paper out and handed it to Karif. "You are selling many records, my friend. Your sales in Britain and in the United States are going up very quickly. It looks like you will be having that US tour quicker than we thought."

Karif looked at the paper in disbelief. "Really?"

"Yes. You are a very valuable property to the record company," Yaroush said. "They were most insistent that I come out here myself to check on you and tell you the news in person."

Karif turned to Gavin and kissed him on the lips. "Is wonderful!" He stood up and took Gavin's hand. "Come, I show you what is meaning."

Gavin stood and followed Karif up the stairs. Yaroush watched them go, then said, "This boy. Who is he?"

I skimmed through the story, smoothing out the rough edges -- that they had met in Houmt Souk when we were shopping, that Karif had asked Gavin to stay at the villa. "He's making Karif happy," I said. "And making it easier to control Karif and keep him out of trouble."

"You have checked his background?"

Liam nodded. "He has a criminal record. But only for small crimes, from being poor and having no opportunities. Aidan and I have been watching him."

"He has stood up for Karif a couple of times," I said. "I think we can trust him."

"Poor men are dangerous men," Yaroush said. "I know this from much experience. I am worried that he will try to take advantage of Karif."

"We're worried too," I said. "But at some point you have to let Karif use his own judgment. Will they be together forever? I don't know. Will Gavin break Karif's heart? Sell him out to a tabloid paper? All possible. For right now, Gavin is very good for Karif."

The mood in the house was much lighter. I spent the afternoon cooking to a soundtrack of Karif's CDs. Yaroush spoke on the phone, the boys went swimming, and then we all sat down to a celebratory dinner. Yaroush warmed up to Gavin, who spoke carefully and refrained from too much roughhousing with Karif.

Yaroush went to bed early, followed soon after by the boys. Liam and I went for a walk outside in the moonlight. We checked in with Luqman, then walked around to the far side of the house where the property looked out on empty acres, the moon shining above.

"I'd like to come back here sometime," I said. "When we can enjoy ourselves."

"You're not having fun?" Liam turned to look at me, a grin dancing on his lips.

"You know what I mean. Yes, I'm having fun. I never thought I'd go riding on a quad bike or kite surfing. And I'm sure there are worse assignments than spending the day sunbathing naked with a bunch of cute guys."

"Be careful," Liam said. "You don't want me to get jealous." He took my hand. "I do know what you mean. But this is what pays our bills, and I think we're both damn lucky we're not cooped up in an office somewhere back in the States, saving all year to spend a few days in a place like this."

We stopped and looked up at the stars. I remembered all those years I had spent wishing on stars, hoping for a life of adventure, excitement, and romance. I stopped when I moved to Tunisia; I couldn't imagine anything more than I already had.

I snuggled against Liam's chest, and he wrapped his arms around me, then leaned down and kissed the top of my head. I hoped that Karif and Gavin could find the same kind of happy ending -- or happy start to a new life together -- that Liam and I had found.

23 — SPREE

The next morning Yaroush asked for a ride back to the airport. "We all go," Karif said. "I take Gavin shopping in Houmt Souk. To celebrate."

"Let's hold off on celebrating until we're sure you're safe," Liam said.

"I think it would be fine," Yaroush said. "Yes, come to the airport with me and then go shopping." He opened his wallet and pulled out a sheaf of dinars. "Consider this an advance on your next royalty payments."

Karif took the money with glee. "We have some fun!" he said to Gavin.

Yaroush sat up front with Liam, and I squeezed in the back of the Land Rover with Karif and Gavin. They were happy and playful, and I had to stop them from giggling and tickling each other. I was relieved when we dropped Yaroush at the airport and I could take the front seat.

"Now, you're on your best behavior, right?" Liam asked Karif as we parked in Houmt Souk. "No running away, no sex in public."

"Best behavior," Karif said.

He led us on a dizzying shopping spree through the markets. The fruit vendors sold us bags of lemons and oranges for juice, and dried apricots and figs for nibbling. From a leather maker, Karif bought vests for himself and Gavin to match the one Liam often wore. "Aidan, you are not wanting vest?" Karif asked.

"I don't have the kind of chest that Liam has," I said, smiling. "But you guys go ahead."

We returned to the same jeweler where Karif had bought the necklaces for himself, Liam, and me. Liam had not been pleased that I'd allowed Karif to make such an expensive purchase for us; he felt that was blurring the lines between client and bodyguard. Even so, he and I had been wearing the necklaces occasionally so that Karif would not be offended.

We were wearing them that morning too. The links of gold were so carefully wrought, so light, and I loved the feeling of it around my neck. "We must have bracelets to match our necklaces," Karif announced as we walked into the souk.

"Not for us," Liam said. "But you should get a necklace for Gavin. Actually, he could have mine."

His hands moved up to unhook the necklace, and Karif immediately took offense. "You not like?" he asked.

"I like it, but it's too nice a gift," Liam said.

"If you like necklace, then you like bracelet too," Karif said, the spoiled brat rising up inside him, the one we had been successful at keeping tamed so far.

"Let's see what they have," I said. Karif and Gavin walked up to the counter, and I whispered to Liam, "Remember? Keep the client happy."

"You just want jewelry," Liam said.

"Yes. But it will make Karif happy to buy something for us."

We joined Karif and Gavin at the counter. They picked out a necklace for Gavin and a matching pair of ancient Roman gold coins as pendants. They were beautiful, worn smooth at the edges. Each had a palm tree at the center, with faded writing around the edge.

"They were meant for trading with the Bedouins," the jeweler said. He was a short, round man, more Middle Eastern than Arab, and he spoke English with a British accent.

"Maybe I have ear pierced," Karif said, pointing at a row of rings.

"Ah, those are not for the ear," the jeweler said. He pointed to his own breast. "For here."

"Oh, I can buy a pair for you," I said, elbowing Liam.

Gavin and Karif turned on him. "Your nipples are pierced?"

They were, though Liam always took the rings out when we were on an assignment. I was sorry about that, because I loved to play with his nipples, licking and sucking them, teasing them with the tip of my tongue. When he had the rings in, I could grab them with my teeth, twist them slightly, and see Liam's body shudder.

Liam was not happy I had revealed his little secret. "We must buy a pair for you and have you put them in!" Karif said. "Which do you like?"

The rings Liam had left at home were simple gold hoops. The ring Karif pointed out was a tiny male figure, his hands raised to hang from the gold ring. I knew Liam wouldn't wear anything like that, and I could see from the way he crossed his arms over his chest that he was not happy with the way things were going.

"How about that one?" I pointed to a gold hoop with a tiny gold ball attached. "I would like that." I looked at Liam and smiled, and I saw his lips inch toward a grin. "Yes, two of those, please," I said.

"And you?" Karif said. "You should have your nipples pierced too."

"Uh, no," I said.

"I have rings for men who do not wish piercing," the jeweler said. He pulled out a separate tray, silver this time, lots of starbursts and wings.

"That one," Liam said, pointing.

Karif and Gavin both burst into laughter. The ring Liam had chosen for me had a clasp at the top that squeezed the nipple, and it had been engraved to look like a padlock. From it, on two silver strands, hung a tiny pair of handcuffs.

"I think that represents your interest in law enforcement," Liam said, holding back a big smile.

"Yes! We will take one of those," Karif said. "But now, back to rings!"

I fell in love with a pinkie ring in the shape of a gold lion's head, and I was calculating how much it would cost and how much money we'd be earning from this gig when Karif saw it too. "We must have four of those!"

"No," Liam said, and I wanted to kick him. "You can buy one for yourself and for Gavin, if you really want. But not for Aidan or me."

"Fine," Karif said, pouting. "We will take two of those."

The jeweler packed everything up, and after browsing through a series of souks that sold handmade pottery, we were ready to leave. I saw Gavin whisper something to Karif, and then Karif said, "Last stop. We are buying clothing. I want new, for me and Gavin."

Considering they had spent a good portion of their time naked by the pool or (presumably) naked in bed, I didn't think clothes were that big a deal. But Karif insisted we walk back to a fancy store in the lobby of the Hotel Grand Djerba.

Liam called Ilias Bouchta and warned him we were on our way, and he met us at the front door. "Welcome back," he said, smiling, his hands outstretched. "I hope you will have better visit than you have had in the past."

He walked with us to the clothing store, off the main lobby, and stood outside with Liam and me as Karif and Gavin shopped. I saw the clothes piling up on the counter, and Liam grumbled, "He's going to need another suitcase to carry all that crap home with him."

Ilias's radio buzzed, and he stepped away. When he came back, he said, "We are hosting a large conference that begins tomorrow," he said. "Many VIP guests -- religious men, politicians, industry leaders. Will you still need my men outside your villa? I could use them here."

"Maybe we could keep one man at night?" Liam asked. "I think we will be all right during the day, but I would rather there was someone at the gate after dark."

Bouchta was pleased. "I will make the arrangements."

"What kind of conference?" I asked, just making conversation while we waited for the store clerk to total up Karif's purchases.

"Yet another on the future of Palestine," he said. "This will be our third or fourth in the last year."

Alarm bells went off in my head, and I could see from Liam's face he was thinking the same thing. "Palestine," I said. "Do you know, perhaps, if a man named Ibrahim Fayed will be here?"

"You know him?" Ilias asked.

"Karif does," I said.

Recognition dawned in Ilias's eyes. "Yes, he is a keynote speaker. His good friend, the imam Hassen Ben Chedi, who instigated the local imam to protest at my hotel, will provide the invocation. They are to discuss spiritual concerns in an independent Palestine."

"I'm sure that makes you happy," I said to Ilias.

He shrugged. "Happy or not, I do not invite the guests. I only protect them."

Karif and Gavin came bustling out of the shop, laden down with bags. "We are ready for going home now," Karif said.

"Why don't you all have a drink by the bar?" Liam said. "I'll get the car. I'll radio Aidan when I'm in the driveway."

"Wonderful!" Ilias said. "Let me take you out and get you a table."

He left us there. "You know Luqman," he said, pointing to where our night guard stood by the pool kiosk in his hotel uniform. "If you need anything, just ask him to arrange it."

I ordered a lemonade, while the boys got fruity bar drinks, and we relaxed under an umbrella by the pool. "We have surprises for you when we return to the villa," Karif said.

"We have a surprise too," I said. "Not a good one, though. There will be a big conference here at the hotel, starting tomorrow. Ibrahim Fayed will be here."

Karif looked down at his drink, sipped, but did not say anything. "Did you already know that, Karif?" I asked.

He nodded.

"Oi," Gavin said. "You didn't say nothing?"

"I am not think it matter," Karif said.

"Not matter!" Gavin said. "Your ex-boyfriend is coming to town, and you didn't tell me?"

"Keep your voice down, please," I said. "Karif, you should have told us that you knew Ibrahim was coming to Djerba. This could make things more dangerous for you." I saw Gavin about to open his mouth, and I said, "And you should have told Gavin too. Communication is important in any relationship." I looked over at Gavin. "Keeping secrets from each other only hurts both of you."

Karif sulked over his drink, and Gavin glared out at the pool. I was relieved when Liam radioed that he was in the driveway. I signaled for the check, which I paid with Karif's credit card, leaving an ample tip. Then we hoisted all the bags and walked back to the lobby.

"You get in the front, Karif," I said as I went to the back of the Land Rover and popped open the hatch. Karif hopped in as Gavin and I loaded the bags and then got into the back together.

No one spoke on the way back to the villa. When we arrived,

Bakri had already left; we assumed Ilias had called him to the hotel to help with preparations for the conference.

Karif hopped out and went inside, not even bothering to help with the bags. "Dizzy queen," Liam muttered as he, Gavin, and I unloaded the car.

"Got that right, mate," Gavin said.

24 – SECRETS

"What happened to our young lovers?" Liam asked when we had carried everything inside and Gavin had gone out to the pool. Karif was up in his room.

"Karif confessed that he knew Ibrahim was coming to Djerba," I said. "I told him he should have let us know. And Gavin was pissed that Karif had kept the secret. As if Gavin didn't have enough secrets of his own."

"You think he still hasn't told Karif about his record?"

I laughed. "Gee, both of them have records. Karif has music records, and Gavin has criminal records."

"What are you saying?" Karif said. I hadn't heard him come to the balcony at the top of the stairs. "Gavin is criminal? You check on him? And not tell me?"

Liam looked at me. "You put your foot in it this time."

I let out a deep sigh. "Come downstairs, Karif. Let's go out and talk to Gavin."

All the high spirits from the morning were gone. Karif and I found Gavin sitting under the umbrella, staring out at the desert behind the house. "It's time to put some cards on the table," I said, pulling up a chair next to him and motioning for Karif to do the same.

"Before we agreed to let Gavin stay here, Liam and I did some checking on him," I said to Karif. "We wanted to make sure he wouldn't hurt you."

Both boys looked angry. "We discovered some things about Gavin's background, and then we made a decision. I stand by that decision."

"What was decision?" Karif asked.

"Gavin is a good guy who has had some trouble in the past. But Liam and I both came to trust him. We decided it was best for him to tell you about his past when he thought the time was right."

I saw tears welling up at the corners of Gavin's eyes, but I didn't say anything more. This was his story to tell.

He did. It was the same story he had told me a few days before, with a few details added, a few subtracted. I still felt he was holding something back, but I didn't challenge him.

When he was finished, Karif said, "I am sorry I am not tell you Ibrahim come to Djerba. I am frightened you are jealous."

"And you should be," Gavin said. "I don't like you seeing your old boyfriend. Makes me crazy, just thinking about you with anybody else."

"There is no other for me, my love," Karif said, reaching out for Gavin's hand.

"I'll leave you two alone," I said, standing up.

"No," Karif said. "We come inside. For fashion show!"

While I told Liam what had happened, the boys scampered upstairs. They were back a few minutes later, carrying a shopping bag and showing off a new outfit each. Both wore sleek dress slacks, Karif's in black and Gavin's in navy blue. Each wore a silk shirt and black dress shoes. "Very handsome," I said.

"Is not all," Karif said. He looked at Gavin, and at the same time they both undid their belts and dropped their pants. They wore cute bikini briefs decorated with funny icons. They wiggled their butts at us, then pulled their pants up. "We bought for you too," Karif said, handing the bag to me.

I opened the bag and found matching bikini briefs for me and Liam, as well as the bag containing our jewelry -- the bracelets and the nipple rings. "You must try them on!" Karif said.

"No," Liam said. "Karif, you are our client. We are here to protect you. We both appreciate your kindness, but enough is enough."

Karif pouted. "You not my friends. Only my employees."

"We work for the record company," Liam said. "They hired us to protect you. You aren't our boss; you're our client."

I knew we were supposed to maintain boundaries between us and our clients, but I thought Liam was going too far. Karif had a lot of emotional baggage and fear, and it was up to us to help with that. And I felt a further obligation -- as a gay man a little older, perhaps a little wiser, with more experience of the world, I wanted to help him, mentor him. If that meant blurring a few boundaries, I could manage.

"Liam's right," I said. "You know we both like you, Karif, and we care about you. But none of us can forget that we are here to protect you, no matter what that means." I held up the shopping bag. "It was very kind of you to buy these things for us. It means a lot to both of us to know you are happy in spite of your problems. And I'm pleased you like us enough to buy us gifts. When we all return to Tunis, and you're safe, I hope we can be friends."

Gavin put his arm around Karif. "He's right, love," he said. "You have to see that they care about you. But they're doing a job now, and you have to respect that. Now let's go back upstairs. We can continue this fashion show in private."

"Nicely done," Liam said when they'd gone. "I was afraid you were going to strip down and put on a bikini."

"You have to admit, we've blurred the boundaries. It's hard for Karif to accept that we can swim naked with him one day, then get all stiff about trying on some underwear he bought for us."

"Stiff?" Liam asked. "I like your choice of words."

I looked down at his groin, and I could see his dick growing and straightening out. "I would like to see you in those briefs. While the boys are occupied, why don't we have a fashion show of our own?"

He came over to me, wrapped me in his arms, and pressed his body against mine. I inhaled his scent, looked up at him, and ran my finger over his lips. They were dry and chapped, but he opened his mouth and took my finger in, and when it was good and wet, I traced it around his lips again.

Then we kissed. I pressed my lips against his, felt their warm pressure back. I snaked my tongue out, and he opened his mouth to receive it. His breath tasted like fruit-flavored gum, and he turned from kissing my lips to breathing against my neck, kissing me lightly there as I arched my back with pleasure.

"I think we'd better take this upstairs before we end up

sprawling naked on the floor," I said.

"You have something against that?"

"Hey, you're the one who was talking about professionalism and boundaries," I said, smiling. I took his big hand in mine and pulled him along, picking up the bag of gifts from Karif in my other hand.

I loved holding hands with Liam. His were bigger than mine, rougher, with thick fingers and clean, close-cropped nails. I twined my fingers with his as I led him upstairs, pulling him back toward me as we went into our room and closed the door.

He was more interested in the bag than in me. He took it from me and started looking through it. "Here it is," he said, holding up the nipple ring with the dangling handcuffs. "You can try this on for me."

I stepped back, unbuttoning the first buttons of my shirt, looking into his eyes as I swayed. Liam licked his lips, and I had a brief flash of him as a hungry wolf waiting to devour me. My dick stiffened and pressed against my shorts.

I undid the rest of the buttons, then slipped my shirt off one shoulder, turning to the side. Liam watched, a big grin on his face. I slipped the rest of the shirt off, then tossed it to the floor. I ran my thumb around my left nipple, teasing it into stiffness. "Hey, that's my job," Liam said.

He took the little nub between his fingers, pressed and tweaked until I felt my legs weaken and my dick start to leak precome. "Now, let's see how this works." He sprung open the clamp, positioned it over my nipple, and then pressed it closed.

218 | NEIL S. PLAKCY

The pressure of the silver against my nipple sent sensations through my body. Liam lifted the two tiny handcuffs and swung them on their thin silver chain, and I groaned with pleasure. He leaned down and took my other nipple in his mouth, sucking and nibbling on it while toying with the handcuffs and their chain.

I thought I was going to come in my shorts before I even got naked. I pushed Liam back. "My turn," I said. "I want to see those new nipple rings on you."

"You do, do you?" he asked. "And what makes you think you're in a position to demand anything?"

I reached out and caressed his dick, stiff through his shorts. "Because you want me. And that gives me power."

I backed away, turned to the bag, and retrieved the two gold rings, each with a little gold ball hanging from the center. "Shirt," I said.

He was wearing a white scoop-necked T-shirt that stretched tight across his formidable chest and abs. He pulled the tail out of his shorts, then raised the shirt up a few inches, passing one flat hand over his abs, holding the shirt up with the other. My mouth watered, thinking of the times I had licked my way over that massive chest.

He pulled at the bottom of the shirt, tugging it up above his shoulders and his head, and I was reminded again of the way his body resembled a Greek sculpture -- the interplay of muscle and rib, the twist of the torso.

He dropped his shirt next to mine on the floor and reached for one of the gold rings. He rolled it in his palm for a moment to warm it up. Looking down, he found the piercing and slipped the ring in. I saw his body shiver and imagined the sensation of metal against flesh. Maybe I'd have my nipples pierced too.

He put the second one in the same way, then put his hands on his hips and stared at me. I stepped close to him, taking the gold ring in my mouth, manipulating the ball with my tongue. Liam shivered as the ring tugged on his nipple.

I played with the other ring with my fingers as I sucked and tongued the first. Then I began to lick my way down the treasure trail of light brown hair that led from his pecs to his groin. "Not so fast," he said, pulling me back. "You've still got some more fashion to show. I want to see you in that bikini."

"In it?" I asked. "Or out of it?"

"In it first."

I backed away, unbuttoned my shorts, and dropped them and my boxers to the floor, then stepped out of them. My dick was stiff and dribbling, and wagged in the air as I bent over to fish the cute briefs out of the bag.

"Let's see," I said. "Karif bought one pair in Large and one pair in Extra Large. Which do you think are for me? Think he knew that my dick is bigger than yours?"

"You screwed around with the ruler when you measured."

"You have the bigger ass," I said, tossing him the XL pair. I bent down and stepped into the briefs as he growled. "Oh, you know I love your ass," I said, looking up and grinning. "More to love and all that."

I shimmied into the briefs, which were pretty tight for a Large. I had to fold my stiff dick in, and even so the head peeked above the waistband. Liam went down on his knees and started licking the length of my dick through the cotton-and-nylon briefs, which molded themselves to the curves of my hips and butt.

Once again we'd found ourselves in the same position: Liam still mostly dressed, me mostly naked. It turned us both on. He maintained a sense of control, and I gave myself up to him totally. He kneaded my ass cheeks with his big hands, pressing the bikini into my crack, sticking his hands between my skin and the fabric.

He pulled down the bikini, now wet with his saliva and my precome, and ran a finger up my dick from the root to the tip. I groaned with pleasure and put my hands on his head, feeling the rough bristle of his crew cut. He wrapped his hand around my dick and started pumping. Sweat began to bead on my forehead, and my pulse rate quickened.

Then he backed off. "Don't stop," I said.

"I have something better in store," he said. "You think my ass is fat?"

He turned his back to me, dropped his shorts, and wiggled his ass cheeks at me. He was wearing his customary jockstrap.

"I think your ass is gorgeous," I said. He leaned up against the wall and spread his legs, and I got down on the carpet. I pulled aside the strap that ran down his ass and began rimming him. Licking first up and down, then folding my tongue and penetrating his hole. I sucked on one finger for a moment, then began toying with his ass with it, teasing my way around the hole, then going in.

He inhaled deeply. "Oh, yeah," he said.

I stood up, pulling his ass cheeks apart with my hands, aiming my dick at his hole. It was too high. "Step back," I directed, pulling his legs wider, lowering his hole to meet my waiting dick. It slipped inside like it had found its home.

I grabbed his hips and started moving in and out of his ass, slowly at first, then gaining a rhythm and accelerating. Liam groaned with pleasure and spit into his hand. He began jerking his dick as I slammed into his ass, both of us panting and muttering and moaning. I caught my breath in a high squeak as my dick erupted up his ass and he clenched his cheeks on me.

His hand moved faster and faster on his dick, and then, before I pulled out, I heard him sigh as he shot off. I reached around his chest, nestled my head against his back, and kissed his shoulder blade. "I love you." I breathed into his skin.

"I love you too." He turned around, and we kissed, and then we stumbled together into bed, leaving the debris of our clothing for the next morning.

25 – RENDEZVOUS

We were eating breakfast, laughing about something, when we heard, very low, a bit of tinkling music. "My phone," Karif said, jumping up. He dashed upstairs to retrieve it.

"It's him," Gavin said. "The ex."

"You recognize the ring tone?" I asked.

"Don't have to," Gavin said. "I knew he'd call."

I was going to say something, but Liam caught my eye, and I decided to keep quiet. Gavin and Karif had to figure out their issues on their own.

When Karif came downstairs, there was something funny about his smile, like he'd been caught being a bad boy but was unrepentant.

"What did Ibrahim want?" Liam asked casually. "To see you?"

Karif's smile deflated. "You were listening?"

Liam shook his head. "Call it a lucky guess."

Karif sat back down at the kitchen table. "Yes. He is arrived in Houmt Souk this morning and wanting meet with me."

"You're not over him, are you?" Gavin asked. "No, you're not. No matter how he treats you, you're just going to keep on going back to him." He shook his head and stood up. "I can't take it anymore. Either you're mine, or you're not. I don't share, and I don't waste my time with guys who jerk me around. I'm packing my stuff and moving on."

He stalked out of the kitchen, leaving Karif openmouthed. I got up to clear the dishes, and Liam pulled the laptop over to him and leaned over it.

"You must help!" Karif clutched at Liam's arm. "Tell him not go!"

"You're the only one who can do that," I said.

"But you protect me!"

"Not from a broken heart," I said, beginning to rinse the dishes. "If I were you, I'd go talk to him. Now, before he finishes packing."

Karif looked from me to Liam. Both of us continued doing what we'd been doing, and he pushed his chair back and left the room.

He didn't go upstairs, though. He went out to the pool instead.

"Guess we're saying good-bye to Gavin," Liam said.

"Shame. But if Karif is still hung up on Fayed, it's fairer all around."

I felt those mother hen instincts but forced them down. I couldn't make Karif love Gavin; I couldn't wipe out his memories of Fayed either. If our calculations were correct, he had begun having sex with Fayed when he was still a boy. Who knew how his psyche had been disturbed by that? He'd grown up without a father and probably found one in Ibrahim Fayed. Ties like that were tough to break.

Gavin came downstairs with his duffle. He walked into the kitchen and lay the necklace, bracelet, and ring Karif had bought him on the table. "Would you?" he asked.

"Why don't you take them," I said. "They were a gift, after all. You might need some cash to get moving."

"Nope," he said. "I'll make my own way."

"Want a ride into town?" Liam asked.

"That's kind, mate. But I need to start getting by on my own again."

I walked over and hugged him. "Take care of yourself, Gavin."

He smiled. "Always have."

Liam stood up and hugged him too. I was so intent on the scene that I didn't realize Karif had come in from the pool.

"Please," he said, his voice choking. "Please not to go."

"You're a good bloke, Karif," Gavin said. "I like you, I really do. Maybe I even love you. But you can't keep looking backward. It's not fair to me."

I stepped over to Liam and took his hand.

"I love you," Karif said. "But Ibrahim too. I am once loving him like you, but no more. He is my past, but not to ignore, or wipe away. You must understand this."

Gavin shrugged. "It's been great, mates." He shouldered his bag and turned toward the door.

"Gavin," Karif said, and his voice broke into sobs. "What do you want?"

He turned back, his duffle still on his shoulder. "I don't want you to see or talk to Ibrahim again."

"I can't," Karif said. The tears were streaming down his face. "He is saying he must talk to me."

Gavin just stared. I couldn't hold back anymore. I said, "Liam and I will be with him, Gavin. You could come too. So you can see for yourself. If you don't like what you see, you can leave. But I think Karif would really appreciate it if you would give him the chance."

Liam looked at me, and I saw a smile quirking up on his face. "Yes," Karif said. "Please, Gavin. Stay. Come with me. You see Ibrahim is man of my past only."

I looked over at Gavin. It was the telling moment; was he willing to stick around for the tough times, or was it his instinct to flee?

He dropped his bag on the carpet and opened his arms. "Come here, you," he said to Karif, who rushed across the room to embrace him.

They kissed, and Gavin wrapped his arms around Karif and lifted him off the floor. When he raised Karif's shirt and put his hands underneath, I said, "Boys! Hello! If Karif is going to meet Ibrahim Fayed, we need to do some advance planning. Which means you need to hold off on the joyous reunion until we get some details."

Liam laughed. "What did I ever do without you to boss me and the clients around?"

I poked him in the stomach. "I'll boss you around later. For now we need some logistics."

We all sat at the dining room table. "When does Ibrahim want to meet you?" I asked Karif.

As Liam used the laptop to pull up the conference schedule, Karif said, "He say he have many meetings. I am calling him later."

"Ibrahim is giving the keynote address when the conference kicks off," Liam said. "Nine o'clock tomorrow morning. So I think our best bet is to set up a meeting this afternoon or evening, before things get busy over there. We'll get in, you can find out what he wants, and then we'll get out."

He nodded toward the phone. "You want me to call?"

Karif nodded and pushed the phone toward him.

Liam spoke at first in Arabic, then switched to English. "Mr. Mahfouz, I'm Mr. Al-Fulan's bodyguard. You make any arrangements with me."

Liam held the phone out so I could hear Mahfouz argue. "Then there's no meeting," Liam said. "You go back and tell your boss that. There is no privacy anymore, not when Mr. Al-Fulan's life is in danger. There will be a bodyguard with Mr. Al-Fulan at all times, as well as Mr. Al-Fulan's assistant, Mr. Jones."

I quirked an eyebrow at Liam. Gavin elbowed Karif. "I'm your assistant now, mate," he said in a low voice.

Karif was as tense as a plucked guitar string. "Yes, I'll hold on," Liam said.

The four of us sat there and stared at each other until Liam held the phone back to his ear. "That works," he said. "Two o'clock in Mr. Fayed's suite at the hotel. I'll let the security chief know we're coming."

It was already eleven o'clock by then, so we had to scramble to get ready. Liam went back to the Hotel Grand Djerba to look around and talk to Ilias Bouchta, and I had to keep both Karif and Gavin calm, which wasn't easy.

Liam returned just before one. None of us were hungry, so we got into the Land Rover and took our time driving to Houmt Souk. Ilias met us at the front door, and as we'd done before, we kept Karif in the car until Liam got out and made sure the area was clear. This time, though, we gave the keys to the valet and we all went inside together, following Ilias through the lobby and down a hallway.

He stopped in front of a double door halfway down the hall. "This is Mr. Fayed's suite," he said as he knocked.

The man who answered was sallow faced, about five-six, with a receding hairline. "My name is Ali Mahfouz," he said in English. "I am Mr. Fayed's confidential assistant. Please come in."

We followed him into the living room of the suite, which had been furnished with a pair of couches, a coffee table, and a few chairs. An armoire stood against one wall, and a pair of sliding-glass doors looked out to a patio and the ocean beyond. The carpet was a thick pile, and the furniture looked elegant and expensive. A door on each side of the room led to what looked like a bedroom and bath.

Fayed sat at the table with papers spread before him. When we walked in, he stood up. "Karif!" he said, and the two of them embraced. Gavin's mouth was set in a thin line.

Fayed looked very much like an important politician in his charcoal gray pin-striped suit, crisp white shirt, and red tie. His black hair was cropped close to his head, and I could see tinges of gray at his sideburns. His olive skin was the same tone as mine, and I was reminded how close the Jews and the Palestinians were -- not just geographically but ethnically as well.

Karif introduced Liam and me as his bodyguards, and Gavin as his assistant. We all shook hands, and then Ibrahim motioned us to the sofa and chairs. As we had choreographed, Gavin walked over to stand by the sliding-glass doors. I went back to the front door, and Liam stood behind the sofa at parade rest. Since he spoke the best Arabic, it was important that he be closest to the conversation. Ali Mahfouz sat back down at the table and returned to his work.

Karif and Fayed switched to Arabic as they sat down. I understood most of what they said; I had a feeling that both were choosing their words very carefully in light of the highly charged situation and all the people around them.

Fayed said Karif looked very handsome and hoped he was doing well in light of all the bad publicity. Karif said he was fine, and that it was good to see Ibrahim again.

Fayed felt it would be best for Karif to leave the Arab world entirely for a while until things had calmed down. I noticed Ali Mahfouz looked up then. Fayed suggested America or Canada, and Karif said he hoped to go on a tour there in the next few months.

Fayed shook his head. "No," he said. "You must go now. You cannot wait."

Why was it so urgent that Karif leave quickly? Elections in Palestine were scheduled in two weeks. If Fayed won, he would become the president of the Palestinian National Authority. Was he eager to get Karif out of sight before someone discovered the truth of their relationship?

They talked back and forth for a few minutes, and then we were all startled by the earsplitting siren of the fire alarm. Liam nodded to me, and I opened the door into the hallway. It was filled with people pushing and shoving as they struggled toward the exit at the far end of the hall.

"We'll go out through the patio," Liam announced. Gavin opened the door for Liam, who stepped outside, his hand on the gun in its holster. I shepherded Mahfouz, Fayed, and Karif toward the door, and at Liam's signal we went out single file.

Once we were out in the sunshine, I looked around. People were streaming out of the exits, all of them shouting to be heard over the fire alarm. I smelled smoke coming from the poolside bar, and Liam pointed in the other direction, toward the kiosk where we had taken our kite surfing lessons. I figured he hoped to rope François into getting us away in his boat.

Liam took the lead, with Fayed and Mahfouz behind him. Karif and Gavin followed them, and I took the rear. I was scared, between the sirens and the smoke and all the shouting, frantic people. I put my hand on my gun and tried to slow my heart rate the way Liam had taught me.

The shots came in rapid fire, as if from a rifle or machine gun. "Down!" Liam shouted, turning behind him. Mahfouz was already dragging Fayed behind a tree as Gavin tackled Karif and took him down. I felt a bullet zoom past me and turned quickly, trying to find the source.

Liam had already identified where the shots were coming from. I saw him assume his shooter's stance and fire off three shots in succession. There was more screaming around us, and the smell of smoke hung in the air. But there were no more shots, and I heard someone blasting out of the underbrush, away from us.

Liam took off after whoever it was. I made sure my four charges were safe and hustled them down the beach to the shelter of the water sports kiosk.

"What is going on?" Mahfouz sputtered in Arabic as I pushed them along. "Where are we going?"

"You need to be safe," I replied in English. "If you want to go back there, go ahead."

"Come along, Ali," Ibrahim said.

We reached the shelter of the kiosk, and François let us into the room where we had watched the kite-surfing video. That seemed so long before, though it had only been a few days.

"Everyone okay?" I asked once we were inside.

Fayed said he was fine and looked over at Karif, who was shaking. Gavin had his arms around him, speaking quietly into his ear, and I could see Fayed recognized what kind of assistant Gavin was.

Mahfouz was on his cell phone, speaking rapidly in Arabic. I had no idea who he was speaking to or what he was saying, but it sounded like he was angry rather than scared.

Liam joined us a few minutes later. "I winged him, whoever it was," he said. "I found blood by the base of a palm tree." He held up a piece of paper, what looked like a photo clipped from a newspaper. "And this."

We clustered around to look at it. It was a photo taken of us all leaving the hotel by boat after the aborted interview with Joseph Saad. I had seen it replicated on a number of Web sites. From the caption I could tell the photo had been clipped from an English-language paper.

It was not surprising that the assassin had clipped the photo and brought it with him. What surprised me, and I guess everyone else, was that the face that had been circled, with an arrow pointing to it, was Gavin's.

26 – INTERROGATIONS

"We don't have much time," Liam said. "The police will be here any minute." He turned to Gavin. "Why was your picture circled?"

Gavin crossed his arms in front of him. "They must have thought I was Karif's bodyguard," he said. "See how I'm the one closest to him? Aidan's up on the dock, and you're at the front of the boat talking to François."

I had to hand it to Gavin; he was a quick thinker. I was sure he was lying, but I didn't want to get into it in front of Fayed and his slimy assistant.

Ilias Bouchta came to the door of the kiosk with two blue-shirted Tunisian police officers behind him. "May we have a word with you, Liam?" he asked.

By then the fire alarm had been shut down and most of the smoke had been swept away by the ocean breeze. "You take Karif and Gavin back to the villa," Liam said. "I'll come back when I'm finished."

As soon as Ilias, Liam, and the police left, Fayed turned to Karif and began hectoring him in Arabic. From what I could understand, he was reiterating his earlier point -- that Karif had to leave Tunisia, leave the Middle East, as soon as possible, before something else happened.

Karif looked helpless. I took his arm and said, "I'm sorry, but you'll have to continue this conversation later. We need to leave here now."

Mahfouz stepped up to Fayed and began speaking to him in a low voice as I led Karif and Gavin back toward the hotel's front door. The last I saw of the two Palestinians, they were walking back to the patio door of the suite.

Ilias had already spoken to the valet, who had the Land Rover there waiting for us. The boys got in the backseat together. "What will happen to Liam?" Gavin asked as I pulled into traffic on the Rue Ulysse.

"Liam has a license for his gun, and he knows a lot of people in the Tunisian police," I said. "Plus he has Ilias on his side. He'll be all right."

I wished I felt as sure as I had to pretend I was for Gavin and Karif. Shooting someone was a serious issue in Tunisia, especially for a foreigner, and I worried that the police would keep Liam locked up for days while they figured out what had happened at the hotel.

The boys were quiet for the rest of the ride, and I brooded. Why had the shooter circled Gavin's picture? I didn't believe for a minute it was because he figured Gavin was Karif's bodyguard. What was Gavin hiding from us?

When I pulled into the villa driveway, Gavin said to Karif, "Why don't we go upstairs and take a nap, love."

"We need to talk first," I said.

I led them into the living room, pointing to the sofa. They both sat. "Liam and I stood up for you yesterday, Gavin. We both said we trusted you, even though we knew you were hiding something. It's time for you to come clean."

"You talking about that picture?" Gavin asked. "I told you, mate --"

"No more bullshit, Gavin," I interrupted him. "Tell me the truth, or I'm going to turn you over to the Tunisian police."

Gavin's face paled, and Karif turned to look at him. "Yes, Gavin. What are you not wish to tell us?"

Gavin sighed. "I didn't think he could find me. But he did. It was that damn picture in the paper."

"Who, Gavin?" I asked.

"I told you I was on the game back home," he said.

"What is mean, please?" Karif asked. "You play a game?"

"It means Gavin was a prostitute," I said. "He did admit to you yesterday that he slept with men for money back in England."

"You understand, don't you, love?" He reached for Karif's hand, but Karif pulled away.

"Tell us why this man shoot at you," he said.

"I had this mate, you see, Stephen. He was on the game with me. Very posh guy, you know. Went to uni and all. He was the one went out to all the high-class clients. Toffs and all. Even an MP."

"Member of Parliament," I said.

Gavin nodded. "Our boss was a bloke named Lenny. Tough as nails, he were. From Manchester. He were into nasty stuff. Drugs and blackmail and all." He took a deep breath. "Stephen saw some things he shouldn't have. How Lenny was blackmailing this one MP. He told me about it, and the next day he was dead. Overdosed, the old bill said. But Stephen never took no drugs at all."

I noticed Gavin's speech was disintegrating as he returned somehow to the prostitute he had once been. "I got scared out me wits," Gavin said. "Lenny knew me and Stephen was mates, and I thought he'd come for me next. So I took off."

Gavin was shaking by then, tears streaming down his cheeks. Karif did not make any move to comfort him, and I thought that was hypocritical. He was little more than a prostitute himself when he was younger, accepting money and gifts from Ibrahim Fayed in exchange for sex.

But Karif had been in love with Ibrahim. Did that make a difference?

"You know Lenny's last name?" I asked Gavin.

"Solbern," Gavin said. He spelled it for me.

While I waited for the laptop to boot up, I watched the boys out of the corner of my eye. Gavin was the picture of misery, sniffling and crying and holding his arms wrapped around his chest. As the laptop came to life, I saw Karif reach one tentative hand out to Gavin, who took it. Neither of them said anything.

I fiddled around until I found the program I was looking for and looked up Leonard Solbern. He was not a nice character, with quite a record. "I need to let Liam know about this." I reached for my cell phone. "If Lenny reached out to someone in Tunisia to kill you, that guy could know where we are."

"It weren't no someone," Gavin said. "It were Lenny his own self."

"What do you mean?"

"I recognized him as we were walking into the hotel. He was standing out by the street."

"And you didn't say anything!" I couldn't help the way my voice rose. "Are you stupid? You saw a man you thought might want to kill you, and you didn't mention it?"

"I weren't sure it was him," Gavin said. "Could have just been some other bloke what looked like him. Plus it would have meant telling you all that stuff, and I knew you had Karif to worry about."

"Suppose Lenny had missed you and shot Karif?" I said. "You didn't think about that? I'm not even expecting you to consider me or Liam getting hurt or killed. We're just the staff to you, aren't we?"

"I'm sorry," Gavin said, sobbing again. Karif moved over and put his arm around Gavin, pulling his head down.

"You are not to yell at him," Karif said defiantly. "He say sorry."

"Whatever." I knew it wasn't professional, but I didn't care. Gavin's stupidity could have gotten any of us killed. I walked into the kitchen, dialing Liam's cell.

"I'm at police headquarters in Houmt Souk," he said. "They've asked me to tell them what happened three times already. Ilias is talking to them now." He paused. "You get back okay?"

"Yup. I have some news for you, though." I told him what Gavin had said about Lenny Solbern.

"What an idiot," Liam said. "All right, I'll pass that on to the police. You stay in the villa. We don't know if this guy knows about it."

"Take care," I said. "I love you."

"Love you too," Liam said; then he hung up.

I looked out the kitchen window toward the pool and the empty desert beyond. Was Lenny Solbern out there somewhere, plotting another attack on us? Would Liam be all right?

I didn't like being in charge, but I sucked it up and went back to the living room. "You guys can go up and take that nap now," I said. "Liam says nobody goes outside until we can track this guy down."

"You are thinking we leave Djerba?" Karif asked.

"We may have to," I said. "But we're not going anywhere until we see what happens with Liam."

"I'm so, so sorry, mate," Gavin said. "I should have told you everything."

"It's all water under the bridge." I shooed them toward the stairs.

While they napped, I tracked down a British guy I'd been in bodyguard school with. When I reached him, I asked for his help in finding out if the police were looking into Lenny Solbern and who I should contact about him.

He said he'd look into it for me. He was a former cop, and I knew he still had connections, so I was hopeful he could come up with something.

Dusk was falling outside, and I'd had no more word from Liam. When I tried to reach him, my call went straight to voice mail, and I wondered if the police had taken the phone away or he'd just turned it off. I made a light dinner, but none of us had much appetite. We all picked at the salad and pasta, and the boys went back up to their room as soon as they were finished.

That left me, sitting in the living room with the lights dim, staring out at the front gate, waiting for Liam.

27 – HAVING A BLAST

Luqman arrived at ten o'clock for his shift at the front gate. He had heard everything that had happened at the hotel from Ilias, but he didn't know anything about Liam or the police department's progress.

I went back inside and sat by the living room window. I tried to empty my mind of everything; worrying about Liam wasn't going to help. He was smart and strong and well connected. I had to believe he'd be all right.

Just before eleven o'clock, a car's headlights began the climb up from the ocean road. I sprinted out the door and was at the gate as Luqman opened it to a police car. My heart skipped a couple of beats as I worried that perhaps the police had come to arrest me or Gavin. But Liam got out of the front passenger seat, thanking the officer for the ride. He, Luqman, and I stood there as the cop backed down the narrow lane.

We left Luqman at the gate and walked back up to the house. "The police are looking for Lenny Solbern," Liam said. "They checked immigration records and discovered he flew into Tunis two days ago."

Both of us were too hyped up for sleep, so we sat in the living room and went over everything that had happened. "If Gavin had been straight with us from the start, he could have told us that he recognized Lenny standing outside the hotel," I said. "Then we could have neutralized him before he got in position to shoot."

"Ilias found a fire in one of the trash rooms," Liam said. "Lenny must have started it and pulled the fire alarm. He had a good vantage point from the place where he was waiting. He had direct sight of both the front and back doors."

"Sounds like he knew what he was doing. Good thing he missed his shot."

We talked for at least an hour, going over possible scenarios. We assumed Karif would want to see Ibrahim Fayed again, to finish their conversation, but neither of us was comfortable going back to the Hotel Grand Djerba knowing Lenny was out there somewhere.

Finally around one o'clock, Liam yawned and said, "I'm going outside to check with Luqman, then go to bed."

"I'll go with you," I said. "A little walk under the stars… you never know what'll happen."

Liam smiled and took my hand. We walked down the drive to the gate, but Luqman was nowhere in sight. "That's strange," Liam said. "He knows what happened earlier tonight. He ought to be right here."

"Could he be on patrol?" I asked.

Liam shook his head. "He'd have heard us and come over."

"I'll get the flashlights," I said.

I was coming back down the drive with our high-powered flashlights when Liam called out, "Over here, Aidan!"

He was kneeling under a date palm a few hundred yards from the gate. Luqman was lying flat on the ground. As I approached, our guard lifted his head groggily.

"Somebody knocked him out," Liam said. "Get in the house and get Karif and Gavin secure; then come back out and help me look around."

I hurried back inside. Karif paled when I told him and Gavin what had happened. "Is someone to hurt me?" he asked. "Or man who is after Gavin?"

"I want you to lock this door, close the curtains, and stay put until Liam or I tell you it's clear," I said.

"I want to help you," Gavin said.

"You can help best by keeping Karif safe and keeping yourself out of the line of fire in case it's Lenny Solbern come back for you. Now lock the door after me."

I ran back downstairs. Liam had dragged Luqman, a skinny, dark-skinned guy with big biceps, up to the front door and left him propped there. "We'll come back to you soon," Liam told him in Arabic. To me he said, "You walk all the way around the house. Be careful, because Lenny Solbern, or whoever knocked Luqman out, could still be on the property. Look for anything unusual -- broken windows, trampled bushes, whatever. I'm checking the outside wall. Yell for me if you find anything."

He loped off down the driveway, and I began a slow survey of the house. I played the flashlight from ground level up, back and forth. There was nothing unusual around the big living room windows or under the balcony from Karif's room. I continued around the side of the house, where the air-conditioning compressor sat on a concrete pad.

I almost missed it. I heard a low ticking noise, and for a moment I assumed it was just the compressor shutting down. But I kept playing the flashlight over the unit, and that's when I saw the small package taped to the side of the compressor.

"Liam! Over here!"

I knew he was nervous because I heard him coming -- usually he walked so quietly he appeared next to me like a ghost. I shone the light on the package. "Is that what I think it is?"

"If you think it's a bomb, then it is," Liam said. "Get Karif and Gavin in the Land Rover and drive them down to the beach. Stay there until I radio you it's okay to come back."

"Gavin can drive. I'm staying with you." I shot off around the house before he could complain.

I yelled up the stairs, "Karif, Gavin, get down here," then scrambled for the car keys. "Take the Land Rover and this radio and drive down to the beach," I told Gavin, grabbing Karif's cell phone from the table as well. "Call the police and tell them we have a bomb on the property. If you see an explosion up here, drive over to the hotel where Ilias Bouchta works. Check in under my name and wait there."

"A bomb?" Karif asked.

"No time," I said. "Get moving." I ran up to the bedroom I shared with Liam and pawed around in his duffle until I found the kit I was looking for. By the time I got back downstairs, Gavin was backing the Land Rover down the driveway.

I hurried to the side of the house, where Liam was on his knees, peering at the package. I handed the kit to him -- it included a knife, a pair of tweezers, and a number of other items for emergency use.

"This is scary," Liam said, looking up at me. "You're reading my mind."

"Knew you'd need this stuff. You figure out what it is?"

"There's a timer inside. That's all I can see until I cut it open."

"Aren't you afraid of cutting wires? Maybe we should wait for the police."

"No time. I'm going to be very careful." He removed the silver pocketknife from the kit. I'd bought the knife in Tunis soon after meeting him, and we had used it several times since then. "Stand back."

I stepped a couple of feet away, shining my flashlight at the package. I held my breath as Liam used the sharpest blade of the knife to slice away the paper wrapping on the package. A big breath escaped me as Liam peeled the paper covering away -- and nothing exploded.

"Okay, bring the light back over here," he said.

A cheap wristwatch, the kind I'd seen in dozens of souks in the market in Tunis, was attached to a larger rectangle with red and yellow wires and duct tape. "What is it?"

"C-4." He pointed. "This wire runs from the watch to the detonator, this little package. At some time, the detonator goes off and then kicks the C-4 to explode."

"Can you disable it?"

"I'd rather have an X-ray machine or a remote robot, but I'll take a bucket of water. Can you get one?"

"Sure." I set my flashlight on the ground, aimed at the bomb, and ran into the house. I grabbed a bucket Alisa used for cleaning, filled it with water, and brought it out to Liam, who was still examining the bomb.

I was sweating like mad by then, and I could see Liam was too, from the way he kept wiping his forehead with the tail of his T-shirt. He said, "On my count, I want you to dump that water over the bomb. The British designed this thing called a pigstick to combat bombs from the IRA -- basically a high-volume water hose that disrupts circuitry. In a pinch you can use a bucket of water in place of the pigstick. With luck, the water will knock out the timer."

I stood over him with the bucket in both hands. "Ready?" he asked. "One...two...three. Dump."

As I poured the water, he snipped the wire that connected the watch to the detonator. The water sloshed over his hands, the air-conditioning compressor, and the concrete pad.

Nothing else happened.

"Okay," Liam said, sitting back on his haunches. "The cops should be here any minute. You radio Gavin and Karif and tell them the bomb's defused, but they need to stay down by the beach till we call them back."

The all-too-familiar siren sounded soon after. It took another hour for the police to look over the bomb, then interview Luqman and Liam. They wanted to know if the bomb was connected to the shooting earlier in the day, but we didn't know. Liam talked to one of the officers who'd been around when the synagogue in Er Riadh had been bombed in 2002. When the police left, he said the officer had made a study of bombs after the explosion.

"He thinks the same thing I do," Liam said. "The bomb looks like ones they've found in Gaza and other parts of Palestine. Hamas use them to blow up people who disagree with them."

"Ibrahim Fayed is a Palestinian politician. You think he arranged something after he spoke to Karif?"

Liam shook his head. "Do I think Fayed is involved somehow? You bet. Karif refused his suggestion to get out of the country, and that could have made him angry. But I don't see how he could get a bomber in place only a couple of hours after their conversation."

"Maybe he knew how Karif would react and he had the backup plan in place."

Liam quirked one side of his mouth in a half smile. "I thought you were the romantic in this partnership. That's a pretty cold suggestion."

"It's a realistic one. In any case, I don't think we should tell Karif about the Palestinian connection. At least not tonight."

"I agree. But this changes everything, you know. We're not safe out here, and I'm not sure we can be. We'll have to talk to Yaroush tomorrow about upping the security level. Maybe we'd be better off taking Karif back to Tunis, or better yet, shipping him somewhere outside the Arab world entirely."

"He and Gavin could go to London," I suggested. "Once Lenny

Solbern is neutralized."

"We'll have to see. Anyway, we need to get them back up here."

I radioed down to Gavin. There was no answer.

Liam shook his head. "This is not good. You know where they went?"

I shrugged. "Down to the beach. Let me call Karif's cell." We went inside, and Liam washed up while I dialed Karif's number. The call went directly to voice mail.

"Shit," Liam said. "I'm going down there. I can run a lot faster than you can. You carry the radio and your cell. If I find them, I'll call you."

He was out the door before I could complain.

28 – LIFE'S A BEACH

By the time I got the radio and the phone and ran out of the house, Liam was gone. An ambulance had taken Luqman to the hospital, and with so much security needed at the hotel, we had no one to replace him. I locked the gate behind me and took off down the long service drive that connected to the beach road.

My feet thudded on the packed sand. Shining the flashlight ahead of me, wiping the sweat from my forehead, I followed Liam's footprints and the tire tracks of the Land Rover. Why had I insisted on staying with Liam and let Karif and Gavin go off without one of us to watch them? We'd been caught shorthanded with Luqman out of the picture; Liam had needed my help to disable the bomb, and we'd assumed Karif would be safe with Gavin. But what if Lenny had planted the bomb as a distraction to separate us from Gavin? We'd sent him to Lenny on a silver platter.

It took me about five minutes to reach the main road. There were no streetlights, no traffic. I waved the flashlight, trying to see where Liam might have gone. On the far side of the road, I saw tracks that appeared to match the Land Rover, and a footprint that looked like Liam's. I started running, following the tracks. I could hear the waves rushing against the shore, but nothing more.

I spotted the Land Rover stopped on the packed sand. Liam appeared from the far side. "They're not here," he said. "But look what they left behind."

As I approached the vehicle, I saw him holding up the radio and Karif's cell phone. "Help me look for tracks," he said.

He went one way, and I went the other. The sand was packed hard, and there was spiny underbrush, so it was hard to spot anything, but I caught sight of two sets of footprints in a soft depression. I called Liam over.

"Where the fuck did they go?" he asked.

I heard something, and I put my finger up to my lips. There it was again --what sounded like laughter mixed with the sound of the surf. Liam took off down toward the water's edge, me behind him. In the glow of his flashlight, I saw Karif and Gavin, naked, coming out of the surf.

"What the fuck do you think you're doing?" Liam said, rushing forward and grabbing Gavin by the arm.

"We're dancing with the tide," Gavin said, laughing. Then he looked at Liam's face, and said, "Oi, mate, you said it was all clear. We thought we'd go for a swim while we waited."

"You freaked us out," I said, catching up to them. "We were worried when you didn't answer the phone or the radio."

Liam released his grip, and Gavin hung his head. "Sorry. Guess we weren't thinking."

"I am sorry also," Karif said. "I am causing so much problems for everyone."

Liam let go of Gavin's arm and stalked back toward the Land Rover. "It's been a tough night," I said. "Come on; let's all go back up to the villa."

I drove the Land Rover, with Liam next to me, not speaking. Gavin and Karif scrambled back into their clothes, both of them soaking wet, and huddled together in the backseat. Without Luqman, there was no one to man the gate, and though both Liam and I were exhausted, one of us was going to have to stay up.

I volunteered to take the first watch. Though I was tired, I had a lot of adrenaline and knew I couldn't get to sleep quickly. Liam could catnap and come back refreshed after just a couple of hours.

"I'll sleep until four, then relieve you," he said, then shepherded the boys upstairs.

Once they were inside, the lights off, I began to shiver. It wasn't cold, and I wasn't wet, but everything that had happened since the morning caught up to me. I rubbed my upper arms, looked up at the stars, and tried to stay calm.

In bodyguard school they had warned us that we might, at some point, feel overwhelmed on an assignment. The best strategy, we had been told, was simply to notify the team leader and ask for another assignment. *"Honesty is the safest policy,"* our teacher had said. *"If you can't do your job, for any reason, you shouldn't jeopardize the safety of your client or your team."*

There were a dozen left in the class by then, of twenty who had started. Eight men, four women. One man and one woman had dropped out because of the physical demands of the course; another two men had failed too many of our written daily exams. The other four had faded away without explanation.

Close protection was as much an intellectual as a physical job.

You had to have the strength and coordination, of course; you had to be able to manage hand-to-hand combat and pass the weapons qualifications. More important was the ability to handle stress, to obey orders, to manage priorities.

I couldn't give up on Liam, though. We were a team, and it was important that I keep up my end. I couldn't be a successful partner to Liam, in any sense, if I couldn't manage the demands of being a bodyguard or loving one. If I flipped out because he disappeared, or was arrested, or put himself in danger, I made things worse.

I took a couple of deep breaths and decided to walk the perimeter of the stucco and stone wall. It was better than just sitting by the gate; at least I'd be active, have something to take my mind off my anxieties.

Moving like Liam did, as silent as a ghost, wasn't easy. It required total concentration on the world around you and was twice as hard in the dark, when you couldn't even see the twig that might snap underfoot, the leaves that would crunch when stepped on.

Back in Tunis I had practiced in the house, in the courtyard behind the bar, and under the trees of the Jardin Habib Thameur. I moved as quietly as I could until I heard a scraping noise. It took me a few seconds to realize I hadn't made it.

What was it? Some animal in the underbrush? I stopped and listened. More scraping, then a grunt.

That was no animal. There was another person out there in the dark with me.

There was no time to radio Liam. I focused on the wall and an olive tree close to it, a few hundred yards from the gate. Someone was climbing the tree, using it as a foothold for a jump over the fence.

This was what had happened to Luqman, I realized. Someone, maybe Lenny Solbern, maybe a Palestinian working for Ibrahim Fayed, had come over the fence to plant the bomb, knocking out our guard. It's funny, but I wasn't scared at all. I just channeled Liam and focused on the task at hand.

I waited in the shadows until I saw a man vault over the wall and land on all fours on the ground. I rushed him, aiming a kick at his chest that knocked him over onto his back, then jumped on top of him, using my knees to pin his arms to the ground.

He fought back, kicking his knees into my stomach and squirming under my grip. I was glad for all the times I had trained with Liam, because I was prepared for everything the intruder threw at me. I banged his head against the ground three times in succession, then felt him go limp under me.

I pulled my belt from my shorts, knocking the radio to the ground. In the dark I couldn't see anything about my assailant. I knew he was about my size and about my strength, but that was all. He roused, took a deep breath and let it out, trying to buck me off.

I pulled his arms up toward me. Quickly I wrapped my narrow leather belt around his wrists, tying it in a tight knot with his hands in front of him.

He was still kicking and struggling with his legs. Fortunately he was wearing sweatpants with a drawstring at the waist. I reached down and grabbed the waistband of his sweats and jerked them down.

He yelped as his dick was exposed to the air. That's what you get for going commando, I thought, smiling. I twisted around, pulled down the legs of his sweats, and tied them in a quick knot. That would immobilize him long enough for Liam to reach us.

I was panting for breath by the time I reached for the radio.

29 – IBRAHIM'S VISIT

Liam burst into laughter as he came running down the lawn to where I stood, shining the flashlight on my assailant, who was on his back on the ground, struggling fruitlessly to get out of the knots I'd tied him into.

"You never miss a chance to get a guy's pants down, do you?" Liam asked.

His T-shirt, shorts, and sandals were wrinkled and twisted from his nap. I was cranky that he didn't congratulate me on my ability to subdue a bad guy on my own.

But I realized I hadn't raved about Liam's ability to wing the shooter at the hotel, or disable the bomb, or any of the things I took for granted that he could do. Perhaps he was starting to think that way of me -- that I had the skills to handle things as they came up. And that meant I really was becoming his partner, not just his apprentice. That felt even better than being able to take down the intruder.

Liam tossed me a cell phone and said, "Call the police. Again." He walked over to the man on the ground. "Well, well," he said, shining the flashlight at the man, who twisted his head from the light. "Lenny Solbern, I believe."

I gave our address and asked for a police car to come out, but when the questions got too complicated for my basic Arabic, I had to hand the phone to Liam.

"How'd you find us, Lenny?" I asked, squatting next to him as Liam finished the call.

Lenny grimaced and said nothing.

"Come on," I said. "One professional to another. You did a damn good job of tracking Gavin down."

"Saw his picture in the paper," Lenny said as Liam was hanging up. "Stupid git. How'd he get a bodyguard job, anyway?"

I laughed. "He's not a bodyguard. Just a very good friend." I sat on the ground next to Lenny as Liam towered above us. "So you saw his picture and tracked him through Karif?"

Lenny nodded. "Untie these ropes, would you, mate?" he said. "I won't go nowhere. Least let me pull me pants up."

"Nope," Liam said. "Not till the police get here."

"How'd you know we were going to be at the hotel?" I asked.

"Thought you all were staying there," Lenny said. "From the caption on the picture. Then I saw you drive away in that Land Rover."

For the first time I noticed Lenny's right biceps was wrapped in white gauze and blood was seeping through it. Liam had winged him. "The Land Rover?" I asked.

"Yeah. Saw the rental-company decal, so I went out to the airport and bribed a clerk to tell me where you had it registered to."

In the distance the police siren approached. They were going to get tired of coming all this way. "Smart guy," I said. "So you came out here...when?"

"You are the luckiest gits in the world," Lenny grumbled. "You never could have tackled me if I hadn't got me arm shot, then busted it up more the first time I came over that fence, when I knocked out your silly guard."

I caught the "first time" and looked up at Liam. He had noticed it too.

"Where'd you get the stuff, Lenny?" Liam asked as the police car turned up our driveway and its headlights shone toward us.

Lenny looked woozy. Blood was seeping out of the bullet wound on his arm, and his eyes were having trouble focusing. "For the bomb, you mean?" Lenny said. "Dead simple." He paused to catch his breath. "You just got to have a few connections in the souk. Dirty place, that. All kinds of nasty stuff you can buy."

I got up to open the gate for the police while Liam stood over Lenny. It took an hour for the cops to hear our story and load Lenny in the car. We both promised to come down to the station in the morning to press charges, and the police car backed down the driveway.

"My watch now," Liam said. "You go in and get some rest."

"You think we still need to worry?"

"I don't know, Aidan. It looks like we've neutralized the threat against Gavin, but who knows who's still out there after Karif. We need to stay focused."

I yawned. "You're right." I leaned up and kissed his cheek. "See you in a few hours."

I thought I'd have trouble falling asleep, but I was out as soon as my head hit the pillow. I woke to sunlight streaming through the window and Gavin shaking my shoulder. "Aidan, wake up," he said.

"What? What's wrong?"

"Police are here. They want to talk to you."

Gavin went back to Karif in their bedroom, where Liam had told them to stay until the police were finished. I pulled on a clean T-shirt and a pair of shorts and went downstairs.

Liam sat at the kitchen table with a middle-aged Tunisian man in a starched white shirt and dark slacks. "This is Lieutenant Chalghoumi," Liam said. "My partner, Aidan Greene."

Chalghoumi wanted to hear from me exactly what had happened the night before, and as Liam got up and made cappuccinos for us, I told him. He had a heavy accent, so it was hard to understand his questions. I was nervous, wanting to be correct in what I said, and I had to stop often and clarify words and thoughts. I went through it all once, then a second time, then a third. We drank our coffee and nibbled on leftover breakfast rolls from the day before, and Chalghoumi made notes.

When he was finally satisfied, he said, "We find hotel key on Mr. Solbern. We search room and find rifle and C-4 explosive. But we must need formal statements from you both. You can come to my station this afternoon?"

Though it was phrased as a question, the command was clearly implied. We both agreed and made an appointment for later in the afternoon. I yawned as I shut the front door behind him.

Gavin and Karif came downstairs and wanted to know what was going on. We summarized quickly, both of us running low on energy.

I saw dark hollows under Liam's eyes too, so I suggested we both go up to bed for a while.

The boys promised to stay in the living room, watching movies. "Don't think it's safe out there just because the police picked up Lenny," Liam warned. "There can still be threats against Karif."

"Got it, chief," Gavin said, saluting. He and Karif snickered, but their smiles wilted when Liam stared them down.

Liam and I stripped and fell into bed, both of us too tired for more than a quick kiss and a snuggle. It was just after noon by the time we woke up, not quite up to full speed but a lot better than we had been. We took quick showers, and as I was getting dressed, I heard Karif singing downstairs.

He had found a small electronic keyboard somewhere in the house, and he was picking out a tune on it as I came to the top of the staircase. "I used to be so sad, dancing all alone," he sang in his clear tenor, accompanying the song with simple notes on the keyboard.

Liam joined me at the top of the stairs, and we listened to Karif sing. "The music of my heart had no rhythm and no tone. Then you came along, and my heart opened wide. You took me to the surf, for dancing with the tide."

Karif looked up and saw us. "Gavin is helping me for writing song," he said. "My first in English."

"It's called 'Dancing with the Tide,'" Gavin said. "Like what we were doing last night."

"Sounds great," I said. "But we're both starving, and I'll bet you guys are too. Let's get some lunch."

We ate at a beachfront café in Houmt Souk and then drove to the police station. We left Karif and Gavin in the lobby, still going over the lyrics for their song, and gave formal statements to Lieutenant Chalghoumi.

That took the rest of the afternoon, and we were all ready for dinner by the time we finished. Instead of eating out, though, we picked up a couple of pizzas to take back to the villa.

After we ate, Karif sang "Dancing with the Tide" for us, accompanying himself on the keyboard. It was a sweet, romantic song, and I had a feeling he had a hit on his hands.

We were relaxing when the house phone rang. Liam answered it. He spoke for a moment, then pressed a button on the phone for a few seconds. Then he hung up. "Ibrahim Fayed is at the front gate. I told him he could come in."

"I am not wanting to talk to him," Karif said. "I am tired of whole business."

"We'll both be right here," I said. "You need to hear whatever he has to say."

Liam answered the door, and the rest of us went into the living room. Fayed came in, followed by Ali Mahfouz. Both of them looked tired.

Karif didn't bother to get up to hug Fayed, just said hello and waved him to a chair. Fayed sat down heavily, while Mahfouz stood behind him. He began to speak in Arabic, but Karif interrupted him. "English, please, Ibrahim. All friends to understand."

"I must make a very deep apology to you, Karif," Ibrahim said.

"Things have been done and said in my name. These things have hurt you, I am sure. Though I had no awareness of them, I feel a great responsibility."

"What things?" Karif asked.

"The imam Hassen Ben Chedi is a very close friend," Ibrahim, said. "He believed that he was issuing the fatwa on you as a favor to me."

"Believe how?" Karif asked.

"I contacted the imam," Mahfouz said. "I was worried that you would continue your foolish disclosures by revealing your relationship with Ibrahim. If such information became public knowledge, it would destroy Ibrahim's chance to make a real difference in Palestine. I thought if you were under a fatwa, you would go into hiding and speak no more to the press."

"You did it?" Karif asked, turning his attention to Mahfouz, who looked down at the floor.

"Not to hurt you," Mahfouz said, raising his head to stare defiantly at Karif. "You are nothing but a stupid boy, like a bug on the window. I must protect Ibrahim."

"That's enough, Ali." Ibrahim turned to Karif. "I have spoken to the imam. He will make a public announcement tomorrow lifting the fatwa. You will be free."

"I never hurt you, Ibrahim," Karif said. "You are good man; you can improve Palestine much. I never tell anyone about us."

"This is sadly not all that I have learned," Ibrahim said.

Ali said something to him in Arabic in a low voice. Ibrahim

turned to him, and they argued.

Liam interrupted. "Are you saying you hired the man who tried to run us off the road on the way to the airport in Tunis?"

That was so long before I'd almost forgotten it had happened. But that incident was the first serious threat against Karif. If our taxi driver hadn't been so skilled, things could have turned out very differently.

Without warning, Ali Mahfouz lunged at Karif. A knife glinted in his hand as he dived toward him.

Gavin was closest to Karif, and he reacted first. He struggled with Mahfouz for the knife and howled in pain as the blade cut him. By then Liam had lunged forward, grabbed Mahfouz by the throat, then pulled him back. The knife clattered to the marble floor, and I grabbed it.

For the third time that day, we called the police to come to the villa. "We should get speed dial," I grumbled. Liam had Ali's hands immobilized behind his back as Ali and Ibrahim argued.

"Ibrahim, you must leave," Karif said suddenly. "Before police come."

"Ali was my assistant, and he acted in my name," Ibrahim said sadly. "I must accept responsibility."

Ali began arguing in Arabic again, but Liam said, "Quiet! Karif is right. Do you have the keys to the car you came in?"

Ibrahim shook his head. Liam reached into Ali's pockets until he found them, then tossed them to Ibrahim. "If you stay here, forget about being president of Palestine and doing good for your people."

"How can I do good for them when I am a liar?" Ibrahim asked. "I have lied to myself, to my wife, to the people who believe in me."

"The only way you can make things right is to go back to Ramallah and lead your people," I said. "What you say to your wife is your own business. But I have read about you and the work you have already accomplished. There is a lot more that you can do."

Ibrahim looked around. No one spoke until Karif said quietly, "Go, Ibrahim. Go now, before police."

With a last look at Karif, Ibrahim hurried for the door. A moment later we heard a car engine start up. I realized Gavin was clutching his side, and there was blood on his hand. "Let me see where he cut you, Gavin," I said.

He lifted his torn T-shirt. The tip of Ali's knife had grazed his skin, but the shirt had absorbed most of the force. I took him to the bathroom, where I cleaned the wound and applied a bandage. By the time I was done, two uniformed officers arrived, followed by Lieutenant Chalghoumi. "I am seeing much of this villa," he said. "Please to inform me you will return to Tunis soon."

"I hope very soon," Liam said. "Now, let me introduce you to Ali Mahfouz."

30 – RETURN TO TUNIS

We did our best to keep Ibrahim Fayed's name out of our conversation with Lieutenant Chalghoumi. The story we presented was that Ali Mahfouz knew Hassen Ben Chedi, which was correct, and that he had felt he was acting on the imam's directive by arranging the attack on us en route to the airport. When circumstances brought him to Djerba, and he discovered that Karif was here as well, he had come out to the villa and attacked Karif with his knife.

There were holes all over the story. "Why did you take this responsibility on yourself?" Chalghoumi asked Ali.

He shrugged. "I felt it was my duty."

"How did you come to the villa? It is much too far to walk from Houmt Souk."

"I took a taxi. But I do not remember anything about the cab or the driver."

Finally Chalghoumi shrugged and directed his officers to take Mahfouz to the jail in Houmt Souk. "We will sort it all in morning."

Gavin said his side was fine, that he didn't need anything more than the chance to hold Karif. The boys went up to bed, and Liam and I did one last check of the gate, where Luqman was back on watch. As we climbed to the second floor, Liam stretched and twisted his back muscles. "My back is killing me," he said. "Sitting out on that cold ground last night did a number on me."

"I'll give you a massage." Blake had sent me to massage school back in Philadelphia so that I could give him professional-quality rubdowns, and that skill had come in handy in our physical lifestyle in Tunisia.

I spread a couple of big towels on our bed, and Liam stripped and lay down on his stomach. I got the bottle of massage oil from the bathroom, pulled off my own clothes, and sat on the bed next to him. I poured oil into my hands. "This was some job," I said as I kneaded his muscles.

His shoulders relaxed as I pressed and rubbed. "You bet," he said, his voice muffled by the pillow. "But we did what we were supposed to do. We kept Karif safe."

"You think he's going to stay with Gavin?" I asked.

Liam mumbled something into the pillow. "I don't know that it matters," I continued. "They're in lust right now. If love comes, that's great. If not, then they'll both move on."

"Says the serial monogamist," Liam said.

I left his shoulders and moved to his lower back, and he groaned. "I'm a big fan of love," I said. "I've been in and out a few times. I love you, and that makes everything in the world better."

"I love you too," Liam said into the pillow, punctuating it with a groan as I used my elbow to work out a difficult knot. I rubbed both his legs, then held his arms out and loosened them up.

"Roll over," I said, backing away.

Liam groaned as he forced himself to turn. His dick was semihard, lolling to the right. I sat down on it as I leaned forward to massage his shoulders. Liam groaned, and I wasn't sure if it was the contact between his dick and my ass, or the massage.

I got my answer quickly as I felt his dick stiffening and pressing against my naked butt. "Mmm," I said, leaning down to kiss Liam's lips. "Not so tired after all."

His tongue tickled the outside of my lips. "Guess not," he said.

I poured more massage oil on my hand and leaned back so that I could wrap a hand around his dick and oil it up. A few slow strokes and his dick was slippery smooth. I slicked his cowl up and down a few times, exposing the mushroom head, and he groaned.

Pressing down on his thighs, I lifted my ass up and positioned myself over him, then ever so slowly let my ass down. His dick slid into me like it had a homing instinct, and my whole body shook with the electric pleasure of feeling him in me.

Our eyes met as I looked down at him and smiled. Balancing my flat palms on his thighs, I began moving up and down on his dick, very slowly, keeping my eyes locked on his. It felt so amazing, having that physical and emotional contact at the same time.

Liam began to push his hips up as I came down, trying to speed up the motion. "You're torturing me," he said, panting. "And you're loving it."

"You bet." But I picked up the pace in response to his thrusts, and soon we were bucking together like a horse and rider in perfect sync. My dick was rock hard, slapping against my stomach as I rode Liam. He grabbed the massage oil, squirted a glob in his hand, and began jerking me.

Once we had our rhythm going, it was awesome. As I rose off Liam's dick, his hand swiped up along my dick, and as I lowered myself down, his hand followed. With his other hand he massaged the underside of my balls, and my body shook at his touch.

His body stiffened under me, and he sped up the action of his hand on my dick. He spurted up my ass with a spasm, and I followed a moment later, shooting off into his hand.

He smeared the come from his hand along my belly. "Big mess," he said, smiling.

"Guess we'll have to clean it up." I wanted to collapse next to him and fall asleep, but I stepped back and grabbed his oily hand. "Come on, lover boy. Let's get in the shower."

He followed me into the bathroom, and as the water warmed up, he leaned me against the vanity, running the tip of his index finger over my lips. "You make me crazy, you know that?" he asked.

"Me?" I asked innocently.

"All my instincts tell me to stay professional on a job," Liam said. "No fooling around, no jokes, certainly no sex. But then you come along, and I'm swimming naked with the client, I'm fucking you where the client can see us --"

"You're protecting the client from nutcases with rifles and bombs," I said.

"Well, that too."

"It's all one life," I said, taking his hand and pulling him toward the shower. "I'm so glad I get to share it with you."

We kissed and hugged each other in the shower, but we were

both too tired to do anything more. We finally stumbled to bed, and I fell asleep cuddled next to Liam, my partner in life and work.

The next morning Lieutenant Chalghoumi told us that the British authorities were eager to get Lenny Solbern, because he had a number of outstanding warrants, and the Tunisian government decided it was easier to extradite him than to prosecute him for the rifle attack on us at the Hotel Grand Djerba or the attempted bombing of the villa.

We stayed in Djerba for two more days until Hassen Ben Chedi lifted the fatwa on Karif and the world moved on to fresher news. Since we hadn't reported the man who had tried to run us off the road in Tunis, the authorities chose to let that offense slide, and Gavin and Karif decided not to press charges against Ali Mahfouz for his knife assault as a favor to Ibrahim Fayed.

Liam and I were both happy to get back to our little house behind the Bar Mamounia, to our dog and our regular routine. We prepared a detailed invoice for the record company, and the day after we submitted it, we met Karif and Gavin for dinner at an Italian restaurant a few blocks from Karif's apartment in Tunis.

"I speak with Yaroush this morning," Karif announced as the waiter opened a bottle of Vieux Magon and poured glasses for all of us. "Colombian singer Shakira have tour of America start next month. She want me to be opening act."

We all lifted our glasses. "Congratulations!" I said.

"I hire assistant look after me on tour," Karif continued, looking shyly across at Gavin.

"Let me guess," I said. "Ali Mahfouz? I understand he's not working for Ibrahim Fayed anymore."

Liam laughed, and Gavin said, "It's me, you prat."

"Well, if you need security on your tour…" I offered.

"My assistant let you know," Karif said, smiling. And then our appetizers arrived, and we got down to the serious business of eating and celebrating.

If you enjoyed this outing with Aidan and Liam, I hope you'll continue with the rest of the series.

The series, in order:

1: *Three Wrong Turns in the Desert*

2: *Dancing with the Tide*

3: *Teach Me Tonight*

4: *Olives for the Stranger*

5: *Under the Waterfall*

6: *The Noblest Vengeance*

7: *Finding Freddie Venus*

8: *A Cold Wind*

9: *The Same Page*

10. *The Madness of Husbands*

11. *The Most Expensive Spice*

12. *The Graveyard of God's Name*

Thanks for reading! I'd love to stay in touch with you. Subscribe to one or more of my newsletters at my website, www.mahubooks.com, and I promise I won't spam you!

Follow me at Goodreads to see what I'm reading, and my author page at Facebook where I post news and giveaways.

If you liked this book, please consider posting a brief review at your vendor, at Goodreads and in reader groups. Even a short review help other readers discover books they might like. Thanks!

ACKNOWLEDGEMENTS

Zoë Sharp's terrific books about Charlie Fox inspired me to write a bodyguard book of my own. As always, I owe a debt of gratitude to all the baristas at Starbucks who kept me fueled with caffeine as I wrote, plotted, edited, and groaned in frustration.

Thanks to all the fans, bloggers, and reviewers who have supported my writing, both in mystery and in romance.

DEDICATION

To Marc: You might think I'm crazy, but all I want is you.

ABOUT THE AUTHOR

A native of Bucks County, PA, Neil is a graduate of the University of Pennsylvania, Columbia University and Florida International University, where he received his MFA in creative writing. He lives in South Florida with his husband and two rambunctious golden retrievers. He is a four-time finalist for the Lambda Literary Award in Best Gay Mystery and Best Gay Romance.

A professor of English at Broward College's South Campus, he has written and edited many other books; details can be found at his website, **http://www.mahubooks.com.** He is also past president of the Florida chapter of Mystery Writers of America.

Printed in Great Britain
by Amazon

45093598R00152